Cloud's End

Cloud's End

Anne Bache

SERENDIPITY

First published in 2005 by
Serendipity
Suite 530
37 Store Street
Bloomsbury
London

British Library Cataloguing-in-Publication data
A catalogue record for this book is available from the British Library
ISBN 1-84394-143-0

Printed and bound by Antony Rowe Ltd, Eastbourne

To my Aunt Mary Bache
who gave me the idea
for this book

Chapter One

It was a damp February evening. The street lights had just come on and each had a yellow halo. The young man in his formal dark coat and pin-striped trousers seemed out of place in this street of terraced houses built of grimy yellow London brick.

He stopped in front of Number 25 and rang the bell. The door was opened by a woman wearing a print overall who had a cluster of improbably yellow curls piled on top of her head.

"Was it about the room love? Because it's just gone! The gentleman is coming in tonight and I couldn't disappoint him. I'm sorry you've come all this way for nothing."

"It's not about the room. I called to see a Miss Anastasia Cloud. Does she live here?"

"Ann? Why, of course she does. This is her home, all the home she has got, poor lass! Are you the gentleman from the Lawyers? We were expecting you but you're a bit too early. She never gets in before half past six. You better come in and wait inside." As she turned to go back in she exclaimed, "There she is! I've never known her as early as this. Perhaps she's ill. Or did she know you were here?"

Mr Peel looked at the girl walking towards them. She was slender with straight, shoulder length, brown hair and seemed withdrawn, lost in her private thoughts. As she approached the woman beside him called out to her.

"You're early Ann. Nothing wrong is there? This is the Lawyer Mr Er … um, the one who wrote to you, you remember. What are we standing here for? Come along in."

Mr Peel met the girl's direct gaze with a slight smile.

"I am Adrian Peel. I wrote to you from Messrs Merryweather, Nebworth and Merryweather. You made an appointment for me to see you this evening."

"Of course. I am Ann Cloud and this is my aunt Mrs Dale."

"Nothing to do with the diary of course." Mrs Dale gave an arch chuckle. "We've already met, love. I thought he had come about the room. You'll be glad to know I let it this morning. Come along in now.

It's cold out here."

She led the way into the living room then turned to face her niece.

"What is it love? Anything wrong at the office? Don't tell me if you'd rather not. Haven't got the sack have you?"

Ann looked up and smiled.

"Right first time!" When she smiled her eyes narrowed to laughing slits and a dimple appeared in one cheek. "Actually I just beat them to it and gave it before being given!"

"Good for you! And then swep'out?"

"And then swep'out!"

Mrs Dale sighed with pleasure for a hurdle safely crossed. "Well I always knew he was a wrong 'un with a name like that! Isn't as if it mattered. Plenty of jobs about." But Mr Peel realized from her tone that jobs had not always been so plentiful.

"I'm not worrying." The girl smiled at her fondly. "Perhaps Mr Peel has come to tell me I have inherited a fortune."

"Hardly that," he observed regretfully. "But, subject to proof that you are actually Anastasia Cloud, there is a house."

"A house!" They both exclaimed at him and he hastened to qualify his statement.

"I'm afraid it is in a deplorable state and there is very little money to keep it up."

"But a HOUSE! I can't believe it!"

Mr Peel produced his brief case and began to take out some papers.

"Come and sit down at the table, and I'll make some tea; but first you must tell us what proof do you need? Haven't I known her since she was born? Her mother was my own sister. I don't know what more you want."

"Don't think for a moment that I doubt you," he said soothingly. "It is just a matter of checking up and producing the papers …"

"What papers?"

"Well, Marriage Certificate, for instance and Birth Certificate – "

"I tell you straight, we haven't got anything like that, have we Ann? What with being bombed out twice, it is a wonder we have anything at all, and none of it is really ours." She gave the ill-assorted furniture cluttering the room a look, which showed plainly what she thought of it.

"Yes, I realize that. Terrible for you! That's why it took us so long to trace you. We can get copies from the public records. It is only a matter of knowing where to apply. You can no doubt tell me where Miss Cloud's parents were married and where she was born. In fact you are a most valuable witness."

"Am I really? I'll be that pleased if I can help Ann to get the house. What about the photo of your father, love? They're as like as two pins, no mistaking who she belongs to."

Ann thrust back her chair and left the room. Mrs Dale drew nearer and whispered rapidly – "It still upsets her you know. Her mother died when she was quite small, and then, when she'd only got her father and fair worshipped him, he has to go and die too. She's got nothing of what belonged to them, that's why it upsets her when you ask for papers. Only that photo – well just a snapshot really, what my other sister took. But it's very like, enough to show Ann belongs."

"I am sure we shall have no difficulty in proving it now we have got in touch with you. It was a different matter when we were working in the dark, with so few clues to help us. That's why it has taken so long tracing you."

"Long? Mean to say you've been looking for Ann for some time?"

"Nearly two years!"

"There now!" she exclaimed. "Wish I'd known! The sooner she gets out of this sort of life the better. She worries me, she does really. Sometimes it seems as if she is only half alive. She's young and pretty – and it's easy for young folks to have fun these days, but she doesn't want it. Since her father died she doesn't seem to want anything any more."

She was leaning across the table addressing him in a fierce whisper. Quite suddenly her eyes filled with tears. "Don't say anything. Just wanted you to know." She flicked her cheeks with her finger tips and turned towards the fire as Ann came into the room. He took the snapshot the girl held out to him.

"Yes, I can see the likeness. Now perhaps you, Mrs Dale, can tell me where Miss Cloud's parents were married and the date so that we can get copies of the certificate."

He was carefully impersonal and business-like, taking down the particulars they were able to give him. As he began to put the papers back in his brief case Mrs Dale asked him:

"Will there be any money for Ann so that she can live in this house?"

It was no good raising false hopes so he shook his head. "Afraid not. The house was occupied by the tenant for life. That is to say, Miss Cloud, according to your grandfather's will your grandmother could live there until her death. After that it was left to your father as eldest son, or, failing him, to you as his heir. All your grandmother's money was left to her other son, Herbert Cloud. It appears that she had no repairs done during the war and since then has not bothered to make up the damage. There is only the rent of a few fields, which go with the house and are let to a local farmer. Probably the best thing you could do would be to put the whole thing up for sale. You never know, someone might take a liking to the place and consider it worth spending a lot on the house for the sake of the pleasant surroundings. No one could live in it as it is."

"Oh? Have you seen it?"

"As it happens I have. I was curious enough to go out of my way after a visit to Mr Hubert Cloud. He has a legal practice at Mallow Greatham. I had quite a job to find the house, which is about eight miles from the market town. It will be difficult to sell unless we can find someone who wants to bury themselves in the country."

"Isn't it called Cloud's End?" Ann asked. "Dad used to talk about it quite often. There was a pool where they caught tadpoles."

"There's your proof!" exclaimed Mrs Dale clapping an emphatic hand down on the table. "You never mentioned the name did you? But Ann knew it from her father. I must say I didn't remember it, although I must have heard him speak of it. But Ann knew it! Shows you doesn't it?"

"Yes, it is quite good evidence," he agreed. "I'm sure you will have no difficulty in establishing your claim. I'll get copies of the certificates and arrange a meeting at the office to get everything tied up."

"That's wonderful, isn't it Ann? We thought her father's relations had disowned him completely, just because my sister was on the stage. It's hard to believe there's folks so bitter and narrow. She was a tartar, old lady Cloud and no mistake."

Ann had been pursuing a thought of her own.

"How do you get there?" she asked abruptly. "Is it far? Could I find it? I should so like to see it before it is sold." After all, it had been her father's home. It was natural she should want to see it.

Forgetting professional caution Mr Peel obeyed an impulse to please. "If you would not mind going on Sunday I could run you down in my car. Take a couple of hours to get there."

"Could you really?" Her delight rewarded him. Her eyes shone and she came alive. "Dad so often talked about it ... it would be wonderful to see it."

Had he thought her insipid and uninteresting? With sudden enthusiasm he found himself making plans for the following Sunday. An early start – a picnic lunch – what if it rains? – who cares if it does?

Mrs Dale watched them, her eyes flitting from one to the other. So prim he had looked in his funny bowler hat, but he was just an ordinary boy underneath, excited and enthusiastic all in a minute. And Ann! It was the first time she'd seemed so keen on an outing. Normally she never expected anything for herself. Surely he would look after her! If you couldn't trust a lawyer – well, anyway, she knew she could trust this grave-faced young man with the smile at the back of his eyes ... She was mentally weighing the merits of white satin against one of these new shimmering organzas, when Mr Peel got to his feet and bade them goodbye.

When she opened the door they saw an extraordinary figure coming up the steps. He had a long black coat and a wide-brimmed black homburg. He was extremely thin and had dark eyes set in gaunt features.

"Well! Fancy you turning up just now!" observed Mrs Dale. "This is the gentleman who's taken your room Mr Peel. Leastwise I know you didn't come about a room after all, but I thought you did. This is Mr Darcy, an old friend of the family."

"Servant Sir." Mr Darcy swept off his homburg then went into the house as they made their farewells and confirmed the arrangements for Sunday.

As Mr Peel walked away it occurred to Mrs Dale that her daughter, Bella, might be interested to meet him. Bella was an actress with an extrovert personality and was quite different from her cousin Ann, although the two girls were very good friends.

At the offices of Merryweather, Nebworth and Merryweather Mr George Nebworth was waiting for his nephew, Adrian, to report on his interview with the 'Lost Heiress'. Anyone meeting Mr Nebworth for the first time and noting the stiff posture, small clipped moustache and crisp speech would correctly surmise that he had been an officer during the war. Mr Nebworth had, in fact, risen to the rank of Major in the Eighth Army. The job of searching for Miss Anastasia Cloud had been passed to him by the solicitor in the small town of Mallow Greatham, Mr Herbert Cloud, who was brother to the girl's father.

The investigations had been time consuming and he hoped that the interview had provided enough information to bring the matter to a satisfactory conclusion so that Adrian could be transferred to more profitable commercial work. Adrian's jaunty entrance into the office seemed to indicate success.

"Well, what's the situation?" He spoke abruptly, without greeting.

Adrian was used to his uncle's manner. "She says her name is Anastasia Cloud although her aunt addressed her as Ann."

"Had she got papers to prove it?"

"No. Apparently they were bombed out during the war. Her father died seven years ago."

"We knew that already. Can we get proof of identity?'

"That should not be too difficult. Mrs Dale, the aunt, was able to give me date and place of the wedding. She also told me where the girl was born."

"Right. Get going and collect the necessary copies. Then we can have her in to clear the formalities and put the case behind us." Mr Nebworth opened his diary and picked up the phone. Adrian wondered whether to leave his uncle in ignorance of the Sunday's expedition but decided it was wiser to keep him informed.

"Incidentally, I have promised to drive Miss Cloud down to Mallow Greening so that she can see the house."

"I don't think that was necessary."

"I know, but she seemed so keen to see the house which her father had loved as a boy that I felt I had to offer."

"Always remember that relationships with clients must be kept formal and impersonal."

"Yes, I know, but I suppose there's nothing to prevent me taking a friend for a run on my day off – Sunday." Adrian left the office without waiting for further comment.

As Mr Nebworth turned again to his diary he wondered whether his nephew was about to enter into an unfortunate liaison with a flighty heiress. He determined to make a point of meeting the girl when she attended the appointment at the offices of Merryweather, Nebworth and Merryweather.

Chapter Two

On Sunday morning the neighbours were treated to the sight of Adrian Peel in his open sports car drawing up outside Number 25. Ann opened the door and stood goggling at the long low car with its hood folded back and its proud owner standing grinning at her. It was not at all what she had expected.

"I hope you don't mind having the hood down," he said. "It's a pity to be shut in on such a fine day." Ann was later to learn that the mechanism for raising the hood on the Marauder was difficult to operate; however, she was happy to enjoy the spring air and was glad to be wearing a warm suit, raincoat and head scarf.

She came down the steps and handed him the picnic basket she was carrying. He stowed this behind the seat and pulled out a brightly coloured tartan rug. "If you wrap yourself in this you'll keep quite warm," he said.

Ann got in and wrapped herself up. She had never been out with a young man in his car before and felt a little nervous. She knew herself to be tongue-tied and shy with strangers.

Adrian was completely at ease. "How do you like my motor?" he enquired as he put it into gear and moved off. "It's very special. Only fifteen of them made. I was lucky to get a good deal from a friend who needed a larger car for his family. He bought a Bentley."

Ann was silent. Few of her friends owned cars, let alone Bentleys.

He glanced at her. "Warm enough?"

"Oh yes thank you. This rug is very cosy."

"We have to keep within the speed limit in the city," he said, as he took the road out west through Hammersmith. "But, once we get into open country I'll put my foot down and you'll be surprised how fast the little bus will go!"

Ann was a bit apprehensive. "Oh please don't go too fast. I want to enjoy looking at the countryside." She then fell silent, absorbed in the unfolding landscape revealed on every rise and round every corner as the powerful car ate up the miles.

Adrian could not help being slightly piqued even though amused at being so completely ignored. He noisily cleared his throat: and, as that had no effect enquired loudly. "Do you smoke?"

She came to with a start. As he suspected she had quite forgotten him. He was no more than the engine driver! However, the face she turned towards him was so alight with enjoyment that he forgave her on the spot.

"No I don't but I'm sure you do. Do have a cigarette or a pipe, whichever you like best. You will tell me when we are nearly there, won't you?"

"We have another hour to go. I hope you won't be bored."

"Oh no! It's wonderful! You can't think how much I am enjoying it all." She turned back to give all her attention to the countryside.

Adrian was content to let her. He began to sing, as he often did when driving alone: first in a bumbling hum, and then in full-throated enjoyment of the sunshine and green fields. Presently he found that she was singing with him. As they worked through a repertoire of popular songs he was glad to be spared the effort of making polite conversation.

"Not far now," he told her as they turned into the market square of a small town. The buildings were an interesting mixture of styles and ages. Shops lined both sides of the square. Ann noticed an imposing grocers, a chemist and a bookshop.

"This is Mallow Greatham where your uncle lives. Those are his offices, look, that brick house on the corner. Did you know he was a solicitor?"

Ann regarded the house he indicated. "Does he live there?"

"Oh no. These are just offices. I should say he must do all the legal work down here."

"Have you met him?"

"Once, when I came to get particulars of the 'Missing Heiress'."

"Did you like him?"

"As a lawyer I should think he is quite sound. As a man – well, no I can't say I did."

"So there is no need for me to get in touch with him. He and my father did not get on very well. This is quite different from London: should you like to have a country practice and live in a town like this?"

And that, thought Adrian, is the first time she has thought about me as a separate person apart from the job. "Yes, I think I should, but you really need to be born to it, and I was born to a London practice. I should be an outsider here."

"Couldn't you get inside?"

"Possibly. After I had been here about forty years they might begin to regard me as one of themselves."

They climbed the hill out of the town up a narrow lane with high banks. At the top they were able to see the rolling hills ahead.

"Oh stop! Please stop!" exclaimed Ann. "Have you ever seen anything so wonderful?" The countryside was spread out before them with a patchwork of plough and pasture, the hedges were starting to be tinged with green and the trees showing the russet colour of swelling buds. The view stretched for miles illuminated by the spring sunshine.

"This is my father's country. He told me about it so many times." Adrian let go the brake and the car rolled gently on into Ann's wonderland.

They travelled for some miles past rough tracks leading to farms with their barns nestling into the hillside. Ann wondered why there were no villages. Then, round a corner, they came to one. A jumble of thatched cottages clustered either side of the road, then came a church and some larger houses.

"This is Mallow Greening," said Adrian.

Ann sat forward, taking everything in. "It's quite a big village. Look, there's a Post Office and a Baker. I think that big one must have been the smithy, but now it's a shop."

Adrian read the headboard. "William Jolly Ironmonger, Merchant, Painter and Decorator. Could be a useful man to know."

Ann was not interested in Mr Jolly. "Which one is Cloud's End?"

"We're not there yet. It's down this lane past the church. Can't hurry, too many bends ..." The hedges were so high Ann could not see a thing. At the top of a small rise they came to a brick wall. Debris of broken tiles from the sagging roof above lay beside it. Adrian turned through a gap in the wall.

"I think this is the back entrance. I could not find the front one. It must have got overgrown." It was easy to understand this as the car pushed past the rhododendron bushes which overhung the track.

"Rhododendrons!" exclaimed Ann. "Won't they make a lovely show in May!"

"They are much too big and will have to be cut right back." Adrian was more interested in protecting his car than admiring the bushes.

They stopped in front of the house which was built in the shape of an 'L' with the solid oak front door set in the middle of the longer side. To the right of the door in the corner of the 'L' was a massive trunk of ivy. Heavy growths of ivy covered most of the right hand wing and much of the main house.

"Ivy does a lot of damage to buildings," grumbled Adrian. "It's a disgrace the way it's been left to take over like that."

Ann was not listening. She had caught a glimpse of water over to the left.

"I'm sure I can see the pool. Do come and look." It was quite a large pool with spikes of flag leaves along one side but clogged with green weed and autumn leaves that had fallen from the overhanging willows.

"Needs clearing out," grumbled Adrian.

"Oh, don't be so dismal. This is the tadpole pond. Can't you hear the frogs grunting?"

"I thought you wanted to see the house," said Adrian as he started to push his way through the bushes by the side of the house. He held the branches back to make it easier for Ann. They came out on a wide terrace that ran the length of the back of the house. This was not so overgrown although weeds had forced their way up through gaps between the stones.

"Now we can see inside," said Ann as she looked through the grimy glass of one of the long windows. "This is a big room. It goes right through the house. How very grand! I want to look at it properly. Do you think we can get inside?"

Further along there was a pair of glass paned doors. "These must lead into the hall," said Adrian, as he tried to push them open without success. "Let's make our way round the rest of the house and see if there are any other possibilities."

All the windows were secure but the back door looked rather rotten.

"I think this must have been forced at some time," said Adrian as he examined it. "Yes, it is now only secured by a padlock with the hasp held on with two screws. I'll get my screwdriver out of the car and soon get it open."

"Do you think we ought to? We might be arrested as burglars."

"There's no-one about, and anyway, it's your house – or will be," said Adrian, as he hurried off in search of the screwdriver.

Ann turned her back on the door and stood looking at the overgrown courtyard and ruinous farm buildings struck by the realization: it's my house. I've been thinking of it as Dad's home but I suppose it really is mine now. Overcome by this stupendous thought she turned to look at her poor neglected property with new eyes.

Adrian's efforts with the screwdriver were successful and soon they were standing in the big room that must have been the original farmhouse kitchen. There was a big old fashioned open range on one side and a row of stone sinks opposite. Adrian commented on the windows set well above head height. "You can see the servants were not meant to waste time admiring the view!" he said.

Ann looked up to the exposed beams in the roof. "It must have been bitterly cold in the winter," she said. "Impossible to heat properly."

"It may have been cold then but it would be wet as well these days," said Adrian. They looked up and could see blue sky through holes where the tiles were missing.

"I hope the rest of the house is not as bad as this," he added. "Perhaps this door leads into it." They went along a short passage and found themselves in a large square hall. There was a stone staircase with an elegant wrought iron balustrade.

"Let's go up," said Ann. She climbed the stairs and walked round the gallery to the door leading to the old part of the house. Along the passage she found what she had been looking for: a small dark room with a window looking out over the old kitchen.

"I remember Dad telling me about this," she said. "They used to drop things onto the old cook and the maids below."

When they had explored the house it was time to think about food. "Let's have lunch on the terrace steps," said Ann. "It will be quite warm out there in the sun."

As they ate Ann looked about her. There was a sizable lawn covered with rough grass that became even rougher at the edges which might indicate flower borders. Beyond was a green field that sloped down to a spinney.

"Is that all the garden do you suppose?" she said. "That lawn would be really nice if it was properly cut."

"That must be a croquet lawn," commented Adrian. "Don't you get involved with that. It's the most vicious game ever invented."

Ann was not interested in croquet. "Do you think there would be a kitchen garden somewhere?" she asked.

"Probably." Adrian leaned back and closed his eyes. "Surrounded by lovely red brick walls, with cherries, plums, peaches and nectarines growing on them … " he sat up suddenly abandoning the dream. "And now with walls tumbling down and everything overgrown with weeds. Horrible!"

Ann smiled into the bottom of her coffee mug. Decay and disorder were obviously his bugbears. He got as cross as if his own property were ruined. She put her mug down on the step. "I'm going to look for it. No, don't come. I shall only peer from a distance."

At the end of the terrace she could see a wall. Were they fruit trees she could see sprouting above it? When she came to the opening she could see a wilderness, there was no point trying to go that way. On her left were steps down to a paved walk through the rose garden. It must once have been very fine but now the bushes had grown into one jumbled mass and the climbers along the wall festooned over them.

Ann managed to walk down the path without getting too badly

snagged. Then she stood on the end of the 'croquet lawn' and looked at the house, her house! It was built of a mixture of red and whiteish grey bricks which gave the walls an intriguing texture. The pairs of tall windows either side of the glass doors shone in the afternoon sunlight. Although she had never seen it before it felt like home. What if she never saw it again? Could she possibly come and live here? Even if it was only for a short time? She walked up to the flower bed below the terrace. There were little shoots sticking up among the weeds. She wondered what they were; daffodils, crocuses, tulips or even lilies. How could she bear never to see them in flower?

"Mr Peel, are you awake? Let me tell you something. I want to come and live here."

Adrian sat up suddenly. Had she really said what she thought she had? Want to live here? With the house in this state! Girl must be mad!

She checked his stuttering protests.

"No, listen, please listen! I don't mean for always; I know I couldn't afford it. But, this was Dad's home, and I want to get to know it and explore all round about before it's sold and I never have another chance. You know I've just lost my job. Well, I don't see why I shouldn't have a few weeks holiday and come and sort of camp out here. It won't do it any harm. If anyone wanted to buy it I could even show them round. I know I couldn't afford it for always, but I've got some savings, I should like to spend them having a holiday here."

The soft hurried sentences surged round him with their urgent appeal.

"But – look here, you couldn't possibly stay here alone, it's simply miles from anywhere."

"It's not far from the village." She was quite practical. "And I shouldn't come here alone. I think I could persuade my cousin Bella to come with me. She is Auntie Lu's daughter, a bit older than me but we get on fine. Let's go inside and have another look."

They made their way back to the broken back door and through the big barn of the kitchen. Adrian noticed a closed door in the passage that led to the main part of the house. "What's in here?" he said as he opened it. Ann went in. It was a modern kitchen with an electric cooker, a stainless steel sink under the window and white painted cupboards and wall units. She opened one of them.

"Look! What treasure!" she exclaimed.

There, on the shelves were sets of plates, bowls, dishes, cups and saucers and a tea pot.

Adrian stood beside her. "I suppose these got forgotten when the house was cleared out," he said. "As they are only plain white war-time utility china they're probably not worth much."

"They would be just the thing for me and Bella when we come to stay here."

Adrian realized that she had quite made up her mind and he had not yet started to point out the difficulties and drawbacks.

Ann was excitedly going round opening other cupboard doors. Most were empty but she found one with a collection of saucepans and frying-pans and a drawer with stainless steel cutlery and wooden spoons.

Adrian opened the door in the blank wall. "Come and look at this!" There, portioned off from the main room, was a fitted bathroom.

"Isn't that perfect!" said Ann.

Adrian saw the possibility of his squashing the mad venture getting more and more remote. Maybe he would be able to enlist the support of her aunt and his uncle neither of whom were likely to approve.

"Shall we have another look at where we are going to live?" said Ann as she led the way to the big drawing room. "This is a lovely room. We shall get the morning and the evening sun."

"It will be a bit cold and gloomy when the sun does not shine," remarked Adrian.

We can light a large fire in the grate. There is sure to be plenty of dead wood around … or … Look! There is a power point for an electric fire."

"You will need that for your television."

"Television! Here? Oh well, I shan't want it, but perhaps Bella will want to keep in touch."

"Why is that?"

"Because she acts in films and sometimes has parts in TV productions."

"Should I know her? What's her name?"

"She calls herself Isabel Duncan. It's a better sounding name than Bella Dale."

"Bella Duncan! – not the girl with fair silky hair who played Rosalind in *As you Like it*? She is a really bright star. You will never get her to come camping out in a derelict mansion."

"How can you say that when you have never met her? Off the stage she is an ordinary person who enjoys adventure. I believe she would come if she possibly could. Think how lovely to be here in the spring and see all the flowers coming out."

"It is too soon to make any definite plans," said Adrian, as he led the way back to the terrace. "We have still got to get all those certificates and things and put them in front of your uncle and persuade him that you are his niece before we can think of opening up the house."

"It won't be really opening up the house, not as you would regard it. We won't have friends down from town or give parties or anything like that. We don't have cars, and we don't drink or smoke or play golf or go riding or any of those expensive things. We shall be able to manage on quite a little you know. We're used to it."

Surprisingly Adrian felt somehow snubbed by her assumption that his life was so different from hers.

"You don't have to starve yourselves." He told her a trifle huffily. "Anyway, I am sure your aunt and my uncle will tell you it is quite impossible. Put the picnic things back in the basket while I go and secure the back door. It is time we started back to London."

Ann felt his lack of sympathy and fell silent. As they pushed through the bushes to the front of the house she broke off a small leafy twig and tucked it carefully away in her handbag as a keepsake.

Chapter Three

Mrs Dale was at the door as the car drew up outside Number 25. Ann got out and waited for Adrian to hand her the basket. She said formally, "I have to thank you Mr Peel for a very pleasant day," and held out her hand. Adrian took it. "We're very formal all of a sudden!"

"It's all so different! You don't understand," she said, and turned and walked into the house and up the stairs.

Mrs Dale looked from Ann's set face to Adrian who was still standing by his car. "What's wrong?" she asked.

He shrugged his shoulders, got into the car and drove off.

Mrs Dale shut the door. "Tea's ready Ann," she called as she went to join her daughter, Bella, in the living room.

As they sat round the table Bella and her mother tried to get Ann to tell them about her day.

"Does Mr Peel drive well?"

"Did you enjoy the countryside?"

"What is the house like?"

"How big is it?"

Ann returned non-committal answers and then burst out – "It's big; a mansion; in the middle of the country. They must have got it wrong. I could not possibly live in it!"

"Well, who wants you to live in it?" said Mrs Dale sensibly. "You have always lived here and welcome."

"The main rooms are very grand; big and lofty with high windows. There are cobwebs in the corners; the windows are dirty with frames that are rotting for lack of paint, and there is no furniture," exclaimed Ann.

"No furniture at all?" asked Bella looking about her at the crowded room. "There is plenty here."

"There is a fitted kitchen with a set of white 'utility' china, but that's all."

"What's the problem? Now you have seen it you can settle down, look for another job and forget all about it," said Mrs Dale.

"That's just what I can't do. I told Mr Peel I would like to go and live there – just camping out with only a bed and a table. But he scorned the idea. He would expect the place to be painted and furnished ready for the 'county' to call before he could live in it."

Bella and her mother had never heard Ann sound so bitter. What had she got in her mind?

"What's the problem?" asked Bella. "Do you really want to go and live there?"

"I just don't know. I heard so much about it from Dad. I feel I can't miss the opportunity of getting to know the house and countryside he loved so much. Once the house is sold I will never get another chance. I can have a holiday there before I start looking for another job."

"Camp out there on your own!" exclaimed Mrs Dale. "A very risky thing to do!"

"It would be much more fun if Bella could have a holiday and come with me."

"You're making a big mistake if you think I am going to miss all my chances of TV work and jeopardize my career," said Bella.

With that the subject was dropped. Ann withdrew into herself and, without much enthusiasm, started looking for a job.

At the end of the week she had a surprise. Bella came back from a morning in town carrying two large parcels.

"I thought we might need these," she said. "Camp beds! I saw them in the Army and Navy Stores going for half price and couldn't resist."

"Oh Bella! How marvellous!" exclaimed Ann. "I presume that means that you don't think I'm so crazy after all. If we borrow a table, some chairs and a cupboard from Auntie Lu we shall have all we need."

"You've got to get it all signed and sealed first, remember, and I shall have to re-schedule things so that I can take four weeks holiday," cautioned Bella. There the matter rested until, some weeks later, a letter arrived from Messrs Merryweather, Nebworth and Merryweather requesting that Miss Cloud call at their office at a time to be arranged.

"I don't know that I want to go," said Ann.

"Of course you must go," said Bella. "I'll come with you to help you stand up for your rights. Besides, I would so like to meet your Mr Peel."

"He's not my Mr Peel," protested Ann. "But, do come; I'll be glad of your support."

The two girls who set out to keep the appointment looked very different. Bella was wearing a smart black suit and Ann her undistinguished tweeds. Once there, Bella took the lead. "Miss Cloud to see Mr Peel," she said to the receptionist. "He is expecting us … er-hum … her," and remembered to push Ann in front as they went through the open door.

Adrian stood up to greet them. "Good morning Miss Cloud I'm so glad …" and he broke off as Bella came to stand beside Ann. She made the introduction. "This is my cousin, Miss Isabel Duncan."

"The 'Beautiful Bella'!" he exclaimed. "You must let me tell you how much I enjoyed your Rosalind."

Bella smiled at him. "Thank you, but I am only here today as 'supporting cast'."

"That's fine, I'm glad to see you. Now I'd better explain that my uncle, Mr Nebworth, wants to be in on this act. All the papers are in his room. Please come with me."

He led the way and introduced them. "Miss Cloud and Miss Duncan, Sir."

Inevitably Bella caught Mr Nebworth's eye. "Saw your Rosalind! Fine performance!" then, turning to Ann, "Well young lady, have you come to take possession? Your uncle, Mr Herbert Cloud, has accepted proof that you are Miss Anastasia Cloud, daughter of Mr Humphrey Cloud and has handed us the deeds and keys of the house. We just require your signature on these papers."

Ann sat at the table and wrote her name where Mr Nebworth indicated.

"Thank you." He then placed another paper in front of her. "And also on this form giving us power of attorney and authorizing us to sell the house on your behalf."

He looked up as Ann stood up, took a step backward and put up a hand as if to ward off a blow.

"But I don't want to sell the house," she blurted out. "At least not yet, not until I have had a little time to get to know the house my father loved."

There was a moment of astonished silence.

"That's put the cat among the pigeons," thought Bella.

"But my dear young lady," stuttered Mr Nebworth. "It would cost a fortune to put the house in order – and the cost of furniture! Quite impossible on the funds available!"

"We shall only use the main part. The roof over that seems to be reasonably sound. We've bought two camp beds and my aunt will lend us a card table and some chairs."

"Could not possibly allow it! They will think you are squatters or some kind of 'commune'. Much better to stay at a hotel or with your uncle!" His phone rang and he lifted the receiver. "Yes I know. He has an appointment. Put him in the Conference Room. I'll be there shortly." The receiver went down with a bang. "This needs a good deal of thought. Come to tea on Saturday. Adrian, phone your aunt and fix it. Goodbye." And he left the room.

While Adrian was phoning his aunt Ann looked at the deeds. "Surely, this is a plan of the house. Does any of this land belong to me? How much is there?"

"About twenty five acres altogether," he said, answering her last question first. Then he came and stood next to her showing the extent of the land.

"How interesting. Can I take this with me?"

"No, it has to be kept with the rest of the deeds in the safe. I could get you a copy made."

"Would that be very expensive?"

"Not too bad. I could add it to our costs."

Ann was still looking at the map. "All this land belongs to me. You said a farmer rents it?"

"That is right. I think there is about a hundred pounds rent owing to you."

"That is wonderful!" A hundred pounds was a fortune to a girl who had never earned more than four pounds a week. "When can I have it?"

"Perhaps on Saturday. I have to get my uncle's signature on the cheque."

Bella had been out of the limelight for too long. "Does your aunt really want to provide tea for two strange girls?"

"She is very hospitable and loves meeting new people."

"Where does she live and how do we get there?"

"You get the tube to Wandsworth Common station and then walk across the common. I'll draw you a map."

"Will you be there?"

"Yes, I have a flat in the top floor of my uncle's house."

Promptly at four o'clock on Saturday they rang the bell of the big red-brick, Victorian house. "Three floors high, and I expect there is a basement as well," commented Bella.

Adrian opened the door and took them into the big drawing room looking out on to the garden. "Here they are Aunt Stella," he said. "Ann Cloud and Isabel Duncan." Ann looked at the smiling face of the elegant lady with her grey hair caught back in a loose bun. We could be friends, she thought as she walked to the window to look at the garden.

Bella stepped forward with her hand held out. "Good afternoon Mrs Nebworth, so kind of you to be entertaining us to tea."

Mrs Nebworth shook hands with Bella then turned to Ann who said, "What lovely crocuses you have!"

"Yes, my garden is my hobby. Would you like to come and look at it?"

"Let them have their tea first," said Mr Nebworth, who had heard the last comment as he entered the room.

"Perhaps we should," replied his wife. "Come along into the dining room." She led the way into the dining room which had a large bay window looking out onto the street. The girls were staggered to see the good things spread out on the table in front of them. "Oh my goodness!" Bella gasped.

"We are just beginning to get back to pre-war standards," commented their hostess. "What would you like to start with? Toasted tea-cake? Or a sandwich? There is salmon, honey or meat paste." Bella set to with a will, chattering brightly with uncle and nephew. Ann had gone very quiet.

"You are not eating anything Miss Cloud!" exclaimed her hostess. "Have a piece of this sponge cake. It is so nice to be able to get fresh eggs again."

Ann cast an anxious glance at her host. "Has he told you I want to spend my holiday camping out in my house? Can he stop me going there?" she said quietly.

"It is not quite so straightforward as that. He has a concern for you and – how can I put it – your father was one of the gentry and he would not want you to be looked down on by people who had been his friends."

"Do I have to meet them?"

"They are sure to get to know you are living there. You will have to go to the shops. Then the nice ones will call and visit you. Come out and see the garden before it gets dark then we will think what can be done." As they went out she asked. "Is there a nice garden at Cloud's End?"

"The garden is badly overgrown, but there were signs of bulbs sprouting. I'm longing to have the chance of tidying it up a bit and enjoying it."

They came back inside to find the others waiting for them in the drawing room. "Now!" said Mrs Nebworth briskly. "Let us have a council of war. We accept that Miss Cloud – may I call you Ann?" and she smiled at the girl. "has the right to go and stay at her house for a time. Do we know if the services are properly connected and useable?"

"We saw some electric plugs but I don't know if the wiring is safe," answered Adrian.

"You better go and find out."

"How can we do that?" asked Ann.

"The first person to try would be Mr Jolly, Builder's Merchant," suggested Adrian.

"Also, the house would look much more civilized with some decent furniture. Shall we go and look upstairs? We have rooms full of things we never use." With Mrs Nebworth in charge objections to the visit seemed to have melted away.

Once upstairs she was in her element. "Carpets make such a difference to the feel of a room," she said. "It will do these good to be unrolled and used. Now, somewhere there is a table and chairs, yes, here they are."

Ann looked at the fine gate-leg table. "We can't take that. We might get it scratched."

'"I am sure that you are capable of looking after and taking care of things. Besides, this is solid oak, not like veneers such as yew which scratch if you so much as look at them." As Mrs Nebworth continued to suggest chairs, cupboards, side tables, cabinets etc Ann realized how much pleasure the lady was getting from planning the furnishing of the empty rooms. "Perhaps we shall be able to arrange for her to pay us a visit," she said to herself.

Although Ann and Bella protested that so much furniture was not necessary to make one room habitable, Mrs Nebworth was insistent. "It will do it good to be used," she said.

As they were leaving arrangements were made for Adrian to take them to Cloud's End on the following Monday.

"My car has a bench seat so three of us can fit in quite easily," he said, but warned them to bring waterproof clothing. "I raise the roof if it is wet but haven't yet managed to seal all the leaks."

"Could put them off for life!" grunted Mr Nebworth, who did not want his nephew to get too friendly with a typist and an actress, even though they seemed to be nice girls.

Chapter Four

Sure enough, on Monday it was wet, very wet, and also cold. As the girls came down the steps of No. 25, with Ann carrying the basket, they looked very alike in their bulky garments. When they were all in the car Adrian unfolded a large waterproof sheet. "Spread this across your laps," he said. "It will keep the worst of the drips off us."

It was quite a different day to Ann's first journey to Cloud's End. Ann sat and looked out at the curtains of rain hiding the view. Bella wondered, as she kept up a lively conversation with the driver, whether this experience would shake Ann's determination to live in the country.

At last they reached Mallow Greening. Adrian drew up outside the 'Old Smithy'. Ann got out, held out her palms, and lifted her face to the rain. "It smells so fresh and clean and sweet, quite different from sooty London rain," she said.

Next to the smithy was the Baker's shop. It had a lovely Georgian rounded window, and two stone steps up to a glass-paned door, which emitted a loud "Ping" as they entered. There was an appetising smell of freshly baked bread and cakes. "Look, at those pasties," said Bella. "Shall we buy one each for our lunch?

"Yes, and let's have some of those jam tarts as well," said Ann.

As she paid for their purchases she asked, "Do you deliver bread?"

The woman behind the counter gave her a curiously examining look from small black eyes. "Well, we do Miss, seeing as there's no other baker in these parts. My hubby, Mr Quickly, does it in the afternoon, but we have to charge extra, what with the price of petrol and everything. Was it for yourself, did you mean?"

"Yes. You see, we shall be living here for a time, and if you could deliver it would be wonderful."

Mrs Quickly picked up her order book. "And the name? And address?"

"Miss Cloud – " began Ann, and continued almost with awe, for this was the first time she had used the words – "Of Cloud's End."

The woman closed the book with a small explosive sound and began to walk away from the counter. "Indeed! We don't deliver there!" There was no mistaking the animosity on her puffy white face. "Good afternoon!"

"Well!" said Bella, as the woman marched through the door at the back of the shop and slammed it behind her. "That's a turn-up for the books! Let's get out of here." Ann said nothing, she had been shocked by the venom in the woman's voice.

Next door they found Adrian talking to a small, spry man in a boiler suit. "This is Mr Jolly," he said. "I've been telling him you want to stay at Cloud's End."

Mr Jolly had dark, twinkling eyes under bushy grey eyebrows. "Welcome to Mallow Greening." He said. Ann relaxed a little. This man seemed friendly. "Thank you," she said, and smiled at him.

"May I say how happy we are to have one of the family at Cloud's End again? I remember your father well as a young man, Miss, you distinctly favour him, if I may say so."

Ann beamed at him, her spirits rising. "Can you tell us anything about the house?" she asked.

"Yes. Mr Peel here has been asking about the electric wiring. I can tell you it is mostly so ancient as to be totally unsafe."

"Oh dear!"

"But," Mr Jolly continued, "when Mrs Cloud was ill she had a new bathroom fixed up downstairs. I expect you saw it." Ann nodded. "And also a modern kitchen with cupboards, sink and an electric cooker. The downstairs wiring was renewed at the same time with points for fires as well as the light fittings."

"What about water?" asked Adrian.

"There's a well, very deep, never runs dry."

"Is the water pure?"

"It never gave Mrs Cloud no trouble, but maybe best if you boil it before you drink it."

"Do we fetch it up in a bucket?"

"There's a pump, manual, semi-rotary. You need to fill the tank every day, good for the biceps." And he rubbed his arm suggestively.

"Did old Mrs Cloud have to work the pump?"

"Oh no! She would never have done nothing like that! One of the village women came in every day to do it, her name is Nellie Crouch. Come to think of it, after all this time it'll need priming. I'd better come and show you. Have you got a key to the house or shall I bring the one I had to do jobs for Mrs Cloud?"

"Mr Herbert Cloud sent us one with the deeds of the house. I've got it here." said Adrian, "Have you got the time to show us where things are?"

"I'll just get a bite to eat and put some tools in the van. Be with you in about an hour."

Once at Cloud's End Adrian opened the heavy oak front door. They were glad to get in out of the rain, which they could hear drumming on the roof over the stairwell. "Last time we were here we had our lunch on the terrace steps," said Ann. "Today we shall have to sit on the stairs." They put their waterproofs in a heap on the floor and made the best of the rather uncomfortable perch.

As they finished Ann noticed water starting to creep past the bottom of the stairs from the passage leading to the old kitchen. She walked up it and opened the door.

"Help!! There's a flood!" she cried. Water was cascading through the holes in the roof until it covered the floor. Although it could not have been more than an inch deep it was starting to flow down the passage towards the hall.

"Whatever are we going to do?" Just then Mr Jolly appeared at the front door.

"What's up?" he asked. "Oh! I see. Let's get the back door open and sweep the water out." He produced two brooms from his van and, between them, he and Adrian removed the worst.

In one corner of the big old kitchen was a pump with a wooden handle. A galvanized tank was mounted on the wall above it."That tank should be OK. Let's try the pump."He worked it up and down several times without success. "We need to tip some water down the pipe to get it going." Water! There was plenty outside – but how? Off a drainpipe?

"What about the pond?" said Ann. Mr Jolly produced a bucket and they soon had the pump functioning. "I hope we did not catch any tadpoles," said Ann.

"If so you'll have frogs in your water tank," said Mr Jolly.

"Oh no!" she was not sure if he was teasing, until a broad wink put her mind at rest.

"I'll show you where the mains switch is. You'll have to advise the electricity company of the meter reading and you're all ready to move in."

"Oh thank you very much," breathed Ann. Adrian handed him his card. "Send the bill to us," he said.

Meanwhile Bella had been exploring ."The through lounge to the left of the glass doors could be an ideal setting for a 'Regency Romance'. I am so glad we are to have Mrs Nebworth's furniture. We need to clean the windows and remove the cobwebs first. We can have our beds in the room on the right and our dining table here in the hall." She seemed to have taken over.

"Whose house is it?" asked Adrian

Bella looked at him. Did he think Ann needed a champion against the 'Bossy Bella'?

When Mrs Dale heard the story of the day's adventures she was very definite.

"You'll be changing your mind now Ann. I am sure a holiday at Southend or Clacton would be much more comfortable and entertaining, and I know this 'house in the country' lark isn't Bella's cup of tea."

Ann looked at Bella. "Would you really hate it?" she asked anxiously. The fate of others besides these two girls hung in the balance as Bella considered.

"Well, today was not very comfortable but I don't suppose it will rain all the time. Also, it's bound to get warmer. Meeting the gentry might give me a lead for some character parts, and, that boy Adrian intrigues me. He is usually so polite and formal, and then an imp peeps out. I'm game if you still want it."

"More than anything else in the world," replied Ann.

Chapter Five

So! Ten days later they were once again in Adrian's car driving through the countryside, only this time, the sun was shining and they could enjoy the sight of shadows from the April clouds moving across the hillsides.

A second visit had been paid to the Wandsworth Common house to try and make sure that they would be having furniture that would be useful without unnecessary clutter. They were not entirely successful in curbing Mrs Nebworth's generosity. "We're only going for four weeks, for goodness' sake!" exclaimed Bella.

The chest of drawers from No. 25 had been packed with holiday clothes and warm jerseys. Suitcases held sheets and blankets and the order from the grocer packed in three large cartons had had to be delivered in his van.

Adrian seemed to have become thoroughly involved in the venture and had insisted on driving them down to take possession. He was no longer "Mr Peel" to the girls although Ann was a little shy of the familiarity of using Christian names.

"We must get the place cleaned up a bit before the furniture arrives," said Bella. "We've got rags and cleaning materials but shall need a broom, a mop and a bucket."

"What do you think Ann? Shall we stop and see Mr Jolly?" asked Adrian; it was her house after all!

"Oh yes, of course, we shall want the rooms we are using to look nice," answered Ann. "We must not be extravagant but I am sure we can use a bit of that hundred pound rent."

Mr Jolly was interested to hear that they were moving in that day. "Is there anything I can do to help you?" he asked.

"Do you know if there is a milk delivery?" asked Ann a bit hesitantly. Their request for bread delivery had been turned down in no uncertain terms.

"We shall need fruit and vegetables as well," said Bella briskly. "Is there a greengrocer here?"

"You should be all right," he answered, "There's Tom Hoby. He takes his van round on Mondays, Wednesdays and Fridays. It's mainly milk but he has a few veg. as well and he'll take orders for anything you want."

"It would be nice if he could come tomorrow, Wednesday," said Ann. "How do we contact him?"

"He'll be calling here in the morning, I'll tell him you'd like to see him."

"Tell him to come to the front door," said Bella.

Meanwhile Adrian had been prowling round the shop and collected a packet of firelighters and some matches as well as broom, mop and bucket. "You'll need firelighters for your fire." he said. Ann added a dustpan and brush and paid for their purchases, and as they left Mr Jolly reminded them of his offer of help.

"I do think that's a nice man," said Ann as they got into the car.

Once they were in the house Ann looked round the hall. "The first thing to do is sweep the floor in here and the other two rooms."

"OK you do that, I'll put the kettle on for some warm water to wipe the tops and cupboards in the kitchen," said Bella.

"What shall I do?" asked Adrian. They looked at him.

"You did your bit driving us down," said Bella.

"We're very grateful," said Ann smiling at him.

He was a little embarrassed. "That's OK, I enjoyed the drive," he said. "Now I'm here I may as well make myself useful."

"Well, perhaps you could use the mop to get all the cobwebs down out of the corners. You'll manage better than me as you're taller," said Ann.

"OK. How wet should I get it?"

"For goodness' sake don't wet it, you'll leave smeary marks. It must be absolutely dry."

They all got to work, and, by the time the van arrived with the furniture, the basic cleaning was complete. Cleaning the windows, polishing the floors and wiping down the walls could be done later. After a busy couple of hours they were able to stand back and view the results of their labours.

Ann looked with delight at the long drawing room. They had only attempted to furnish the area in front of the fireplace. Here one of Mrs Nebworth's carpets, of faded pinks and blues which accorded well with the pale green of the walls, was drawn up to the white marble kerb. To the left stood a chintz-covered couch with a large screen behind it, on the right was a deep armchair, while four smaller chairs with damask seats stood ready for the gentry to call. Against the wall on the right of the fireplace was a glass-fronted cabinet, opposite was a bookcase: there was also a small occasional table with a fluted pie-crust edge. Seeing it as one entered, one end of the room looked exactly right. The other was bare but partly masked by the screen.

"Would it be better to have everything spread out more?" mused Ann.

"Impossible to make it look furnished with what you have here," said Adrian. 'You've done the wisest thing to concentrate it in the one area before the fire. What furniture you have is just right. It makes you realize how elegant the room must have been when the family lived here."

The hall was more sparsely furnished. The table and chairs had been placed in the centre on the largest of the carpets. Next to the door was a strange object. It had a round metal base mounted on three feet. Above the feet were three posts supporting a circular frame, radii to the centre held a tall pole at the top of which was an arrangement of coat hooks.

"Wherever did that come from?" Bella had asked when she saw it being carried in.

"Oh, that's for the gentry to put their hats and umbrellas on when they come to call," said Adrian flippantly. "But I'm sure I don't know where my Aunt found it."

"It can stay there. We can hang our anoraks on it," said Ann. "We're not expecting any gentry." Adrian seemed to be treating it as a joke, she was not quite sure why he should do so.

"I'm hungry," said Bella. "Let's have a fry-up, sausages, eggs and bacon. You'll join us I hope, Adrian?"

"Rather! You're not the only one feeling hungry." He slipped out through the glass doors into the garden while Bella and Ann went into the kitchen. Ann was laying the table when he came back into the hall. He was carrying bundles of dry twigs and branches. "Whatever have you got there?" she asked.

"I thought we should celebrate with a fire in the drawing room for us to drink our coffee by. I knew we should find a use for those firelighters," he said as he went through the drawing room door. Ann sighed. "We've only just swept in there, and I'm sure he'll make an awful mess."

However, when she and Bella were sitting together on the big settee with their mugs of coffee watching Adrian lighting the fire she had to admit that crackling flames would give a feeling of homecoming and celebration.

Adrian put his empty mug down. "It's time I was going. It's been a really great day."

"It really has," said Ann. "I can't thank you enough for all your help."

"Don't mention it. I've enjoyed it. And, before I forget, I've a present for you from my Aunt." He went out to his car and came back with a brown paper parcel, which he gave to Ann. "Aunt Stella thought you might find these useful." Ann untied the string and folded back the paper. "Goodness!" she said as she looked at the small hand-fork and trowel and the secateurs.

"She thought you would need these to tidy up your garden. They're not new, just spares that she does not need."

"What a kind thought. Please thank her for me." The words seemed formal but her shining eyes showed how much the small gift meant to her.

After Adrian had gone the girls sat watching the embers of the fire die away. Ann shivered a little. She suddenly felt very tired and lonely.

"What's up? Are you cold?" Bella asked, her words echoing in the big bare room.

"I suddenly thought; here we are alone in this big empty house, doesn't it feel lonely. I've never done anything like this before."

"It's a bit late to get cold feet now," said Bella sensibly. "You wanted to come and stay in the house where your father lived and now you have. Make the most of it."

"I don't think it was like this when he lived here, so empty and echoing. All the rooms would have been furnished, upstairs as well as down; there would have been family and servants; the house would have been alive."

"And now you think it's dead. Perhaps it is a bit spooky, but old Mrs Cloud lived here alone remember. Snap out of it girl! You're very tired. You'll feel quite different in the morning."

"Oh Bella! What would I have done if you hadn't come?"

"You don't think I would have missed an adventure like this do you? And we've another adventure to come. I've never slept on a camp bed before!"

Chapter Six

There is a certain technique needed in order to sleep comfortably on a camp bed. No-one had shown them the best way of folding the blankets nor told them it was important to have double the amount under than over. After a certain amount of experiment Ann managed to roll her blankets round her into a cocoon and was soon sound asleep. Bella was not so lucky and, eventually, gave up the struggle and had to find slacks and a jersey to reinforce her blankets before she was warm enough to sleep. They were awakened by a loud banging on the front door.

"Goodness!" said Bella. "Do you think that's the milk? I suppose I had better go as I have clothes on." Ann gave a sleepy grunt and snuggled down in her nice warm nest. Bella opened the door to see a man about to get back into the van, which was standing on the drive.

"Are you Tom Hoby?" she called. The man turned "Yes, Bill Jolly said you wanted milk. When there was no answer I thought he must be mistaken."

"I'm sorry. We were both fast asleep. Could we have two bottles please and will you call again on Friday." She took the milk and went back into the house. "That was the milk," she told Ann who looked at her and started to giggle.

"What's the matter?"

"Look at yourself; bare feet, nightie hanging out over your slacks, hair all on end and a blanket round your shoulders." Bella was not amused. She liked to present a smart appearance."He'll spread it round the village that we're a pair of waifs!" she said.

"Never mind, we'll just have to be sure we're properly dressed when he comes on Friday. Look what a lovely day it is. Let's get dressed quickly and go and explore, I'm longing to see if the daffodils are out." For Ann, who was impatient to get out, the chores seemed to take a long time. Bella lingered over breakfast, and it seemed to take forever to fill the water tank. Throughout their stay the girls were to find the morning pumping session a bind, although, as their arms got stronger, it took less time to fill the tank. They learnt to save all the dishes and only wash up once a day, and think twice before they turned on a tap.

"We never had this problem in London," said Bella. "Even during the war the taps never ran dry."

"They did during the bombing you remember," said Ann.

At last they were able to open the glass doors and step out on to the terrace in the spring sunshine. Round the edge of the lawn there were daffodils showing yellow amongst the weeds and rough grass.

"Last time you came it was so wet you didn't see anything, Bella," said Ann. "Let's go and see if there are flowers on the fruit trees in the walled garden." Sure enough, they could see white blossom over the top of the wall, and, once at the doorway, they could not resist the temptation to try and scramble between the brambles and nettles to have a proper look inside. There were fruit trees all round the walls and a parallel row of green bushes down the centre of the neglected plot.

"Look," said Ann, "I do believe there were box hedges enclosing the beds. I wonder if we could clip them to shape again?"

"How long do you think you are going to be here?" asked Bella. "You'd need weeks to tidy this part, let alone the rest of the garden. Let's go and see what else there is."

The bushes in the rose garden were starting to sprout and the ornamental trees in the shrubbery between the lawn and the pool were bright with shoots in all shades of spring green.

"It all wants tidying," said Bella. "Wherever do we start?"

"Start by the house and work outwards I think. Would you like to clip back those bushes along the path from the terrace to the drive?" It was Ann's garden. She wanted to plan the work. "I'll start clearing away the weeds in the borders round the daffodils."

This was the start of a quiet, contented time working in the garden during the day and cleaning the house after dark. As they worked they talked. It was a time away together from their work-a-day world. Each learnt about the other's thoughts and feelings, their philosophy of life, their aims and dreams. Ann was surprised to learn about Bella's doubts and difficulties; getting started in the theatrical world has never been easy. Whilst Bella began to admire Ann's quiet determination to make the most of the opportunities that came her way.

When Tom Hoby came to the door on Friday morning he was met by two young ladies. Admittedly they were informally dressed in slacks and jerseys, but they had silk scarves round their necks. Their faces were discreetly made up and their hair silky and neat. They bought potatoes and greens as well as the milk and asked if he knew where they could get logs for the fire.

"Well, I don't know but Mr Richard Brent who lives at Shallowford Farm might be able to help." Ann fetched her purse and paid for her purchases. He seemed a bit surprised and Bella commented on this after he had gone. "Do we get the impression that old Mrs Cloud did not like parting with money?" she said.

The following morning, looking equally fresh and neat, they set off on foot for the village.

"Do you think they'll stare at us?" asked Ann "I'm not really sure I want to go."

"Nonsense! We can't live here and never go near the place. Anyway I want to see it. The people could be some character studies. Besides we are running short of stores." This sensible advice had its effect.

"I suppose it won't hurt us if they stare," said Ann doubtfully. "Anyway we are not here for ever."

Bella was city bred. "I don't think much of walking along these rough country lanes," she said. "What we need is a car, I wonder if we could afford to hire one? No? Well, how about bicycles? I bet Mr Jolly could hire us a couple of bikes then we could really go exploring."

"It's a long time since I rode a bike," said Ann. "How about you? Do you think we should manage?"

"Once you've got the knack I'm sure you never forget – anyway, we can practice on the drive to get our confidence back." They chattered away and turned the corner into the village, without realizing how close they were, to find themselves among the locals going about their morning activities.

They called at the grocers, cashed some money at the post office and found the butcher, Mr Sprite, whose size was in complete contrast to his name. He was very ready to supply them with anything they required, and to deliver it – of course Miss – and call for an order at the same time.

They seemed to feel smiles and friendliness around them as they walked up the village and were able to relax. Then they came to the baker's shop and remembered Mrs Quickly. "What about bread? We must have bread and there does not seem to be another shop."

Bella refused to be intimidated "I'll go in. She can't refuse to take my money." Ann had not long to wait outside. Bella was soon back outside with a loaf in her hand. "No problem!" she said briskly.

They found Mr William Jolly checking lists at his counter. He greeted them with real friendliness and, although bound to ask gloomily if anything had gone wrong, was obviously enthralled at their account of all that had gone right.

"Bicycles!" he exclaimed. "That is certainly an idea! No; I have none for hire at the moment, but I can easily get some from Mallow Greatham, I'm going in this afternoon. I know where I can find bicycles for hire and will pick out two that I think are reliable and not too expensive and bring them along to Cloud's End tonight in the van."

"Oh, thank you so much," said Ann. "But you don't have to drive out again. We can easily walk into the village on Monday morning and collect them."

"No trouble!" he assured them; so they left their shopping for him to bring out that evening and set off back to Cloud's End very satisfied with their morning. As they walked up the drive they saw a curious figure standing by the front door.

It wore a man's cloth cap, a long brown coat with a fur collar and heavy boots of a farm labourer. It was tall and thin with a long nose in a narrow bony face and regarded them with an inimical stare.

"What is it?" muttered Bella. "Man or woman? Take your choice!" As they reached it, it spoke with a high voice and they realized it was an old woman.

"You'll be wanting some help," she asserted without preamble or greeting. "I used to do for the old lady and I could manage to come for an hour or so and see you right in the mornings. Yes, I could do that. Not as I 'ant got more'n enough to do up at mine, and with a man too, nobody can't know how much work that don't make for me, up at five every morning, us agriculturals know what it is to work hard, us do!"

She flung up her head to regard them balefully from beneath the peak of the cap. "But I can make time for you, you don't want none of they girls from the village, lazy good-for- nothing madams, take your money and what have you got to show for it? But you can rely on me, yes. you can that, used to do for the old lady, get here at seven, light the fires, pump the water and scrub the stone floors while she's lying there in her bed!" with a loud sniff. "But I know how to work, yes, I shall suit, and we don't need to quarrel about the money do we?"

"Oh , please stop!" protested Ann, appalled at the spate of words, so hard to hear and harder to understand. "We do not want any help in the house, I'm afraid, I'm sorry – but we're not actually living here, you know, we only – "

"Not living here? And Tom Hoby asked to call on his rounds with milk and veg. – well, that's a masterpiece!" And she gave a shrill crow of laughter. Her manner, assertive, contentious, and at the same time cringing, was definitely odd. Could the old lady – Mrs Cloud – really have employed her? It was hard to believe. They had to push past her to get the door open and enter the house. Then they were no better off, for the old woman followed them in and sat herself down at the table. Her pale eyes in their hooded cavities darted round the room, and she gave a loud sniff.

"Wants doing," she pronounced. "I could tell you wasn't workers you two, many's the time I done it for the old lady. Well, when shall I come?"

Ann offered up a prayer for strength. "Not at all thank you." She said firmly. Bella regarded her with awe – good for her! Ann was angry. This old woman was attempting to bully and dictate terms to her in her own house and she was not going to have it!

"We do not want any help in the house thank you. We are only staying a short time, so it is not worth a lot of bother."

The old woman was nonplussed, she cupped her hand round an ear and leaned forward: "My affliction makes me that 'ard of 'earing I can't rightly tell what you do say, Miss. But you'll need somebody, and you'll do better with me than with one of them madams from the village. I shan't ask so much neither."

"That's another thing," continued Ann raising her voice. "We can't afford to have someone to work for us; I have not got enough money."

Still with her hand about her ear, the old woman peered at her uncertainly, and Bella realized that she really wanted the job ... Because she needed the money or because she had always worked here? She had been confident she could bully them into giving it her, and was just realizing she had failed. Had she been clean and attractive they still did not want anyone, but somehow it seemed worse to refuse her when she was so very unattractive.

"No money?" The old woman got to her feet seeming less tall than she had appeared at first. "That's what they all say! Starve you they would. All the same they are and the old lady the worst of the lot!" She gave Ann a challenging look. "Well, happen you might want someone later on, I'll be ready." And she stalked out.

"What a scarecrow!" exclaimed Bella. "Come on, I need a drink. Would you like a cup of hot sweet tea – for shock?" Ann began to laugh, and next moment, they were both shrieking together and wiping tears from their eyes. "And that cap," gasped Bella. "If I could remember all the words she used I'd make a wonderful act out of it! Do you suppose your grandmother ever employed her? I can't believe it!"

"I don't know, I can't make out what she was like," confessed Ann. "I hate her for how she behaved to Dad, yet, I feel she must have loved this house, and that makes me sympathetic towards her."

"Let's take our lunch onto the terrace and sit in the sun," said Ann. "I feel some strange body may walk in here at any moment, they are not so likely to find us the garden side of the house."

As they sat on the steps in the sun they noticed a small furry shape creeping towards them through the long grass. "Look Bella!" said Ann quietly, "Do you see a little animal over there?"

"I think it's a kitten," said Bella. "Don't frighten it. I'll go and get some milk." She slowly stood up and went into the house. When she came back she found Ann sitting on the bottom step stroking the kitten with one gentle finger and talking to it in a soft musical voice.

"My goodness!" exclaimed Bella. "I never knew you were a 'Lion Tamer'!"

"I just called him and he came to me," said Ann. "Isn't he sweet? I wonder where he came from? There are no houses anywhere near."

"It just occurs to me that our friend the scarecrow might have left him."

"If so it was kind of her."

"Probably just wanted to get rid of it. Kittens are two-a-penny. Cats breed like rabbits."

"Oh, don't say that, I think it's so soft and cuddly. I've never had an animal before. When Dad was young he had all sorts of animals – dogs, guinea pigs, cats, horses, as well as the farm animals."

"I suppose it will be OK to keep the cat while we are here," said Bella. "But what about when we go back home?" Those two words "back home" echoed in Ann's mind. Where is my home? She wondered. She had found that, to her, home included a garden and there was no garden at No. 25.

Bella looked at her surprised at her silence. "Oh well! I suppose there is no harm in keeping it pro tem. I expect we will be able to find someone to look after it when we leave."

As they were finishing their evening meal Mr Jolly drove up in his van and, true to his promise, unloaded two bicycles. "I've hired them for four weeks," he said. "It was not worthwhile getting them for a shorter period." Hire for four weeks made a big hole in the money they had got out of the post office that morning, but the bikes were going to be a great asset if they wanted to explore the country.

"Now tell us about the old witch who came to see us this morning," said Bella, and she gave a lightning sketch of their visitor; the high reedy voice, the heavy walk, the hand cupped about one ear.

Mr Jolly was delighted! "You've got her, Miss, to the life! Nellie Crouch from Cloud Common! Bitter old varmint! Don't you have her around!"

"Well, we told her we wouldn't, but I would never be surprised to find her down on her knees scrubbing the floor one day. She seems to have got a personal interest in it."

"They get like that, these old tartars! She did for Mrs Cloud for years, on and off, when they weren't having rows. Got the nicest old husband you'd find in a lifetime – and don't she lead him a dance!"

Ann changed the subject. "After that old woman Nellie Crouch had gone we found a kitten. Do you think she could have left it by mistake?"

"No mistake, Miss, if you ask me. Her old mother cat is always having kittens. Nellie has unloaded them all round the village. You don't want to let her get away with it. Shall I take it back to her?"

"Oh, but it's a lovely little animal. I want to keep it. I've never had a pet before." So, regardless of the consequences, the kitten was given a home, fed with tinned meat and milk, and put to sleep in the big old kitchen in a carton lined with Ann's oldest cardigan.

Chapter Seven

On Sunday morning they tried out the bicycles. Ann was so confident that she decided to cycle into the village and attend the morning service. She had accompanied her father to church and knew the Mallow Greening church would have been familiar to him.

She arrived as the five minute bell was ringing and, once inside, was welcomed by a man in a well-cut grey suit with fair hair and blue eyes who smiled at her and handed her the service books. Ann chose a seat at the back and was able to relax in the quiet ambience of the church. As the prayers and the psalms of the well known service of matins proceeded she felt as if her father was beside her and she started to think about her life since he had left her. Up till now she had just drifted along, surely she ought to decide on some purpose and strike out for herself as Bella had done; but not, definitely not, a stage career.

The vicar mounted into the pulpit, tall, elderly, with scanty grey hair, he surveyed the congregation benevolently. Then he started to speak about the story from St Matthew's gospel where the righteous were commended because they gave food and drink to the hungry and thirsty, made friends with lonely people, welcomed strangers and visited the sick and those in prison. "My friends, this is important because it gives us guidance as we go through life. Maybe we are fortunate in having no needy people without food or drink in our village but there are many who are lonely or ill living alone who would be thankful for visits and offers of help. And we are told to welcome strangers, newcomers to our village. I ask you to be sure that you always do this with an open mind; be welcoming, be friendly, and enjoy the adventure of making friends with those who come from a different world." He continued to talk about troubles in the wider world where Christians could provide an example for others to follow and concluded, "I would remind you of the first two verses of Hebrews chapter 13 – Let brotherly love continue and be not forgetful to entertain strangers: for thereby some have entertained angels unawares. I ask you to go out to your daily lives keeping these thoughts in your minds."

As she stood to sing the final hymn Ann found herself wondering if she and Bella were considered to be strangers in a foreign land. A little embarrassed, she put her book down and slipped out to be away before the rest of the congregation left the church.

They had their lunch on the terrace in the sun. When they had finished Ann said, "Come down the field with me, and see if the brook runs along the bottom. I keep meaning to go and explore but we always seem to be doing something else."

"You go love," advised Bella, gathering up the debris of their lunch. "I'll keep an eye on things here and clean the windows. Don't go too far, and if you let out a yell I'll come to the rescue."

Ann grinned at her and set off. The boundary between field and garden was a ditch with a wall supporting the garden. Her father had told her this was called a 'Ha-ha', she remembered this and wondered what the strange name signified. There was a stile in the form of a ladder down the wall, she climbed down and walked down the slope to the line of trees and bushes, which she hoped might hide the brook. She was right. It curved round the bottom of the meadow, turned away and vanished between steep banks much trodden by cattle. There was no sight of a farm, which must have been hidden among the trees. She decided to leave further exploration until Bella was with her, and wandered along beside the brook. She found so much to enjoy, the noise as it tumbled down a small fall of stones, the stillness where it widened into a small pool, birds flying into the bushes, a magpie chattering, and a pigeon hurtling out of a fir tree with a bang, which startled her. Ann had lived all her life in the city, but she had spent whole days, and every holiday, in the country with her father. He had taught her to observe and cherish everything in the countryside. She was only now realizing how exiled and homesick he must have felt. In the middle of a little coppice she found a treasure – a wild blackthorn bush covered with white blossom, which seemed to sparkle against the blue of the sky. She reached up and broke off some twigs. They would look nice in a jar on their table.

In a trance of happiness she walked back across the meadow, a slim figure in slacks and a jersey with a bright scarf round her neck carrying her twigs … and was hailed by a loud and imperious voice demanding furiously "What the hell do you think you're doing in my wheat? Get out of it do you hear? Get out at once!"

Ann came too with a start, and looked about her. Leaning on the gate at the top of the hill was a tall male figure waving angrily. Was he shouting at her? She turned and walked towards him. He continued his tirade.

"I suppose you come from some town and think you're entitled to trample down the crops, leave open the gates, break down trees, dam up streams, frighten the cattle and leave broken bottles about to lame them. You think everything in the country belongs to you, don't you? Well, let me tell you, you are trespassing on my property and damaging my wheat. I intend to report the matter to the police."

Ann heard out this tirade in silence. She was now near enough to see that her accuser was a rough-haired young man in denim jeans and an open-necked shirt with sleeves rolled up to the elbows. While he, seeing her approaching up the slope, had supposed her a child, probably accompanied by other children: and now realized she was not the sort of person to be bawled at.

They gazed at one another with hostile eyes. Ann found herself making excuses "I'm sorry, I had no idea it was wheat. I thought it was just grass."

"And, if it was just grass, you still had no right to walk over it. You're trespassing."

Ann never argued, and now her instinct was to walk away in silence without giving battle; but, somehow, her new status as property owner would not permit it.

"Well, considering this is my land, I really don't see how I can be trespassing."

"Your land! I would like to know what makes you think that! And, even if it was your land, I should still tell you to keep off it."

Ann gave him a look of keen dislike. "I shall try and avoid doing any damage, of course, but I have no intention of keeping out of my own fields and, if you object, I suppose I shall have to give you notice to quit." She was astonished at her quite unexpected courage and delighted to see that he looked taken aback. Then he startled her with a shout of laughter.

"Well! I'll be damned! I've rented this land from Clouds for years now and this is the first time anyone has ever ..." He broke off short, regarding her keenly from widening eyes, and then slapped a hand on top of the gate.

"Of course! You must be Miss Cloud. I knew Tom was delivering milk at the house but thought it was just a short let. I didn't realize the family was living there!" He grinned at her looking suddenly younger and more approachable. 'So I've been bawling at my landlady! Do forgive me I had no idea!"

"Of course not, how could you?" she agreed coolly. "I'm sorry about the wheat, but I, too, had no idea. Having lived in a town all my life, naturally I don't know these things.'

"Does that rankle? But, honestly, if you knew the trouble we have every summer with hikers and campers and what-have-you from the towns: I can't begin to tell you the damage they do."

"Please don't. I can guess! But perhaps some of us will learn in time!"

He gave her a wry look. "I didn't mean anything personal! Have I annoyed you? Look I'm sorry. I apologise." He rubbed a hand through his hair, which did much to account for its appearance. Ann had to accept this apology, but she was still wary.

As usual, her instinct was to retreat. "It was my fault after all," she conceded. "I'll be more careful in future, and walk round the edges instead of going across the middle."

"I notice you still intend to walk in the fields."

"Of course I do," she told him firmly, "It's why I've come here after all." And, with a nod of farewell she walked away, leaving her tenant to wonder how it was that they had got off to such a bad start.

Ann climbed the stile into the garden and sought out Bella who said, "Put the kettle on, will you there's a love. I'm dying for a cuppa." Then, catching sight of Ann's face, "What is it? What's happened?"

"Well, I suppose it's funny really, but I'm not laughing!" remarked Ann who was still seething with anger. "I've been warned off my own land by a farmer who hates everybody who comes from the town."

"Of all the nerve! Who does he think he is?"

"He's my tenant; I told him I'd give him notice to quit ... and I've just remembered that, actually, we're living on his rent so it's a bit awkward! He also supplies us with milk. You can't say we've had a very warm welcome so far!" said Ann sadly.

"No, they do seem to resent us for some reason. Is it because we come from London? Or is it more personal? I don't like to say this of your old granny, Ann, but do you think it's because of her?"

Chapter Eight

Monday morning the postman made the arrival of their first letter quite an occasion by banging the knocker on the front door and presenting the letter with something of a flourish.

He was an elderly man with a thin weatherbeaten face and bright blue eyes.

"For Miss Cloud?" he queried looking from one to the other: and, when Ann held out her hand, "You'll excuse me, Miss, if I say I am very glad to meet you. I well remember your father, Miss, when he was a boy round here."

"Oh, do you? How nice of you to tell me!" Ann gave him a radiant smile pleased that, contrary to most people, he mentioned her father instead of her grandmother.

"Aye, and you're like him, Miss, I can see that," he nodded at her. "I been a postman round these parts for nearly fifty year now, and there are not many that I don't remember. I'm surely glad to be bringing letters to Cloud's End again."

"What a lovely welcome!" said Bella. "We shall look forward to you coming with our letters, although I don't think we are likely to get many."

"You never know, Miss, I might be bringing you a winner one of these days." He gave her a funny little bow and turned back to Ann. "That's from your uncle, Miss. You'll excuse me, but I couldn't help knowing seeing it's got the name on the back. Should you want to send him a reply, you just stick the letter in a front window, and I'll pick it up on me rounds this afternoon. That's what they was always used to do. Good day to you both."

Ann turned the letter over and read the firm's inscription on the flap. This was the first direct communication from her father's world. She took out the letter with some reluctance.

My dear Niece, it began. I have just heard from Messrs Merryweather, Nebworth, and Merryweather, that you are in residence at Cloud's End, where I am afraid you will be very uncomfortable, as the house is in such a bad state of repair. My wife and I would be very glad if you would accept our hospitality for as long a time as you wish to stay in the neighbourhood. This will give you an opportunity of visiting the house from comfortable quarters at not too great a distance, and at the same time, give us all a chance of getting to know one another which we should much welcome. Yours very sincerely, Herbert Cloud.

In silence she passed the letter over to Bella, who read it with exclamatory grunts.

"Typed, and on office paper ... pretty stiff but I don't suppose he can help that! I think he means to be kind! What will you do?"

"Thank him and refuse."

"Are you wise? After all, they are your relations, and this is definitely an opening. You may not get another!"

"Why should I worry? Thanks to you and Aunty Lu I've managed all these years without him, and I don't see why I should put myself out for him now. Just suppose I had to go and stay with them! How ghastly! We have only got such a little time to enjoy ourselves here, and I'm not going to waste it on him!" And her reply, hastily written, although adequately polite, showed a rather too obvious unwillingness to be involved. Bella hoped this would not mar any possible future contacts, but did not think that much goodwill existed to be damaged by Ann's actions. She wondered if Herbert Cloud would be perceptive enough to make allowances for initial shyness; she doubted it but was not going to make any further efforts on his behalf.

Ann propped the letter in the window according to instructions, and thought she would feel better when it had actually gone and she could put the whole thing out of her mind. Then her attention was caught by the filthy state of the windows. The girls had spent their time so far on the sunny side of the house and done nothing in the front.

"Anyone calling will think us very slovenly if they see the windows in this condition," she said to herself, as she hurried inside to fetch water and cloths. Once the bottom panes were clean she realized she needed more height to reach the rest so fetched one of the dining room chairs. She was standing on the chair and stretching to the full extent of her arm to reach the top pane when she heard a voice.

"That looks a bit dicey! Mind you don't fall. A ladder would be better for the job!"

She thought she recognized that voice; yes, sure enough, it was the angry farmer. A swift look round confirmed that fact but did not give her time to take in the friendly smile on the young man's face.

"I would use a ladder if I had one, but a chair works quite well," she said. The chair wobbled as she turned back to the window.

"Do be careful, you'll hurt yourself if you fall."

"I can look after myself, thank you! What are you doing here anyway?"

"Thought I would deliver the milk instead of old Tom, and see if you really did live here. I now see that you do."

"Why should I bother to lie about it?"

"Probably to score me off."

"No! That's too much trouble! I prefer just to ignore you."

"Oh, I see! So you're like the rest of the Clouds and won't mix with low class farmers!"

"I don't know the rest of the Clouds but, speaking for this one, I certainly don't want to mix with anyone so ... so ... absolutely boorish!" She jumped off the chair and walked off round the corner of the house with her chin in the air.

He stood with a bottle of milk in each hand watching her go, the smile wiped off his face. How had that happened? He had come to make friends and bring the firewood she wanted. The row had blown up in two minutes flat. He was too young to realize the difficulty created for future friendly relations by bad first impressions. The softly, softly approach needed to overcome a bad start was not very easy for a man with Mr Richard Brent's aggressive temperament.

The front door opened and Bella marched out. "What have you been saying to Ann?" she asked fiercely.

"Don't worry. She gave as good as she got!"

"It's not like Ann to do that. You must have upset her!"

"I didn't intend to! Honestly! I came to make friends and bring some wood for your fire. Tom Hoby said you were asking for some."

"She said you accused her of being 'stuck up' like the rest of the Clouds. She could not be more different. It's upset her."

"OK! I apologize. Now can you give me a hand unloading this wood. I need to get back to the farm."

Bella talked as they transferred the wood from the van to the porch by the front door. "How could she be 'stuck up'? She has never had anything to be 'stuck up' about! You have to understand that Ann left school at fourteen to become a shorthand typist working in an office – the lowest of the low – at everyone's beck and call; make the tea; post the letters; count the petty cash, even sweep the floor at times."

"He turned to look at her, "That sounds dreary!" he said. "Has she always done that?"

"Well, obviously, it gets more interesting as you get older with more responsibility. You may get to be secretary to a partner or a director; but that's not always easy. They are not all nice men. She had to leave her last post; and not before time too!"

Richard had been absorbed by his own problems for so long it came as a shock to him to realize that others could have troubles. "I see! And now?"

"There is this house she has inherited. It's a different world. She is thrilled to see where her father grew up; and her greatest delight is working in the garden and seeing things grow. I don't know how she will be able to bear to go away and leave it all!"

"Leave? Why should she?"

"I have to be in London for my job. She can't stay here on her own. And, anyway, there's no money."

"No money?"

Just then Ann came round the corner of the house with the kitten cuddled in her arms.

"Look Bella!" she said. "He let me pick him up and likes me to hold him. He's purring!" Richard was struck by the happiness in her face as she looked up. He restrained a sudden impulse to go and put an arm round her shoulders. That would only make things worse!

"Miss Cloud, I apologize if I said anything to annoy you," he said. "I brought the load of wood that Tom Hoby said you had asked for."

"Thank you very much. How much do we owe you?"

"It's about 30 shillings; one pound ten shillings."

"Bella, could you go in and get my purse."

As Bella went in Ann felt the need to make conversation.

"That's my cousin Bella," she said. "Did she introduce herself? Isobel Duncan is her stage name."

"And I'm Richard Brent and live at Shallowford Farm," he said, and broke off fearing to make any further comment that might be taken wrongly.

Bella came back. "I'm afraid there's only nineteen shillings and sixpence here," she said.

"Just like old times! Mrs Cloud's purse was always empty!" His thought sprang out of his lips before he could check it; he could have bitten his tongue out!

Ann went white. "The reason we are short is because we paid Mr Jolly for four weeks bicycle hire. I shall go to the post office this morning and bring the ten shillings and sixpence to Shallowford Farm and … and … THROW it at you!" she said fiercely as she turned and walked away.

This plan of action was put into effect. Ann was able to post the letter to her uncle at the post office. Cycling back they took the right hand fork before the house and freewheeled down the slope to the brook. The other side the bridge was an old farmhouse with thick rough walls painted white and dormer windows under the thatch.

"This must be Shallowford Farm," said Ann. "Wait here while I take the money." She had put a ten shilling note and a sixpenny piece in an envelope and did not really intend to carry out her threat to bombard the young man with coins. As she reached the door it was opened by a woman wearing a large white apron.

"You must be Miss Cloud," she said. "Mr Richard said you would be coming. He is out on the farm but asked me to tell you he was sorry if he seemed rude."

"Who are you?" asked Ann.

"I'm Mrs Bunch. I was nannie to Mr Richard when he was small and now I keep house for him." There was a soft country burr to her voice as she continued. "Mr Richard was telling me about you as he ate his lunch. I've known him since he was a small boy and could tell he was really unhappy about the things he said to you. Now, will you come in for a cup of tea?"

Ann liked the motherly look of this woman but Bella was waiting. "No thank you. My cousin and I are just off to explore on our bicycles. Where does this road go to?"

"Keep straight on up the hill and you will come to Greening Common. You get a good view from the top."

Ann thanked her and they set off on a voyage of exploration.

Chapter Nine

Cycling is good exercise, but it is a little unwise to go too far the first time out. When Ann and Bella woke the next morning they were both suffering from stiffness in thighs and calves and distinctly tender bottoms!

"It must be all those hills we cycled up!" said Bella.

"I think we should have a quiet day on our own in the garden," suggested Ann. "We can put our working clothes on and potter about doing easy jobs."

They were about to get up from the table after a leisurely breakfast when there was a knock on the door. "Another visitor?" queried Ann as she went to open it.

Their visitor had the dark eyes and fair complexion typical of a redhead. She wore a wide brimmed straw hat to shade her face from the sun, a greyish blue knitted cardigan and navy skirt and had sandals on her feet.

"Hello! I'm the vicar's wife, Mary Heriot. Ernest, my husband, asked me to call. Are you Miss Cloud?"

"Yes, won't you come in? Can we offer you a cup of tea or coffee?" They ushered her into the drawing room while she went on talking.

"No thank you. It's not long since breakfast. I'm not sure how to say this – but – Ernest only heard last night that Miss Cloud was in church on Sunday when he preached that sermon about welcoming strangers. He was most concerned that you should not think it was aimed at you."

"Well, wasn't it?" said Ann. "We are strangers and we feel that people stare at us when we go into the village."

"Yes, we had heard talk about two strange smart young ladies and their young man in his smart sporty car coming to live at Cloud's End, so Ernest thought he ought to remind people to be friendly; but, it was not until Lord David Mallow Hampton told him that you had been in church and left early that he was afraid you might be offended."

"Lord Mallow Hampton!" exclaimed Bella, "I've never met a Lord!" Ann ignored her as she tried to explain to their new acquaintance what their situation really was. "I inherited this house but I can't afford to live here. My cousin, Bella and I are just camping out for a short holiday so that I can get to know the house and countryside that my father loved. We have been lent the furniture in this room and the table and chairs in the hall and we are sleeping in camp beds in the dining room."

"I see! Do I remember hearing that old Mrs Cloud had a modern kitchen and bathroom installed in the servants quarters?"

"That's right! They have made all the difference to us. Did you know Mrs Cloud?"

"Yes! and a more cantankerous old ..." she broke off flushing scarlet. "I'm so sorry! I should not have said that! Ernest would be horrified! I'm not really cut out to be a parson's wife!"

Bella's eyes sparkled! "You don't need to mind us," she said. "We know she is the reason people don't want to be friendly. There's Mrs Quickly in the baker's shop. She will only sell to us if we put hard cash down on the counter beforehand."

"Bertha Quickly has been very outspoken about her problems. She claims that there were a lot of bills unpaid when Mrs Cloud died. But the solicitors told her they had no evidence the money was owing so they could not pay her."

"I suppose the solicitor was my uncle Herbert."

"Yes, I'm afraid he has the reputation of being close fisted!"

"I don't think its fair that they should judge me because of them!"

"And, we have had a visit from that old woman Nellie Crouch," continued Bella. "She wanted to come and scrub our floors. Then there is the 'angry farmer' who shouted at Ann to get out of the field – her field."

"Angry farmer? Do you mean Richard Brent? He can be a bit forceful but I am sure he would never be rude. His troubles have made him feel the whole world is against him."

"Troubles?"

"Yes; I don't know the details but his father was found out on the farm with his gun beside him. That was while Richard was at school. Then he got engaged and the girl jilted him for an older man with much more money. I think he was well out of that. She wasn't the right girl for Richard. Too hard boiled. He needs someone more sensitive that he can look after and care for." There was a short silence, then she continued. "Here am I passing on the village gossip when I really came to meet you and welcome you to Mallow Greening. Do tell me, what have you been doing while you have been here?"

"Working the pump to fill the water tank!" said Bella grimly.

"Oh Bella!" protested Ann. "That doesn't take long. There's plenty of time to enjoy the garden."

'"And you do enjoy the garden?"

"It's wonderful! I never had a garden before. It's so nice to see the spring flowers coming. I've tried to clear the weeds away but I don't know if I have done right and I am longing to know the names of all the plants."

"I expect I could help you there. Shall we go out and have a look?"

Ann led the way down the terrace steps and showed their visitor the partly cleared beds. "I've tried to get the grass out because I knew that was wrong but I don't know which of the other plants are weeds."

"There are some nice things here." Mrs Heriot was down on her knees beside the border. "There is campanula, blue or white they are both pretty; here is sedum, the grey foliage is nice in flower arrangements and butterflies love the flowers in late summer. You have got primulas too, these will soon be in flower. And, look! Here are poppy plants. I wonder if they are pink or red. I do so enjoy painting the bright flamboyant flowers. I warn you I shall ask you to pick some for me."

Ann was pleased to find another garden lover. "Did you ever see the rose garden? It is all overgrown but it must have been lovely. I don't know how to tackle the wilderness."

"Let's go and have a look."

When Bella came to call them in for a cup of coffee she found the two enthusiasts discussing the best way of cutting back the undergrowth.

"Have you got a big garden?" asked Ann as they walked back towards the house.

"Not as big as this and mostly vegetables. My husband grows vegetables, I think men prefer them. I spend most of my time painting; flowers, landscapes and portraits. I have a studio upstairs and, once I get started, I forget everything else, it is so absorbing. I'm afraid I am not much use in the parish."

Maybe not; but she was able to tell them about the village, the people, the surroundings and the church. She had strongly individual views and kept the girls entertained with her comments. When she rose to go they felt they had made a friend.

"I will tell Ernest what nice girls you are. Quite different from … you know who. Perhaps you will knock on the vicarage door next time you are in the village. I will show you my paintings and our garden." She wheeled her large upright antiquated bicycle away from the wall and rode off with a wave of her hand.

In the afternoon they had another visitor. Ann was sitting on the grass at the bottom of the steps playing with the kitten and Bella had just come out with two mugs of coffee. This visitor had a solid no-nonsense look about her. Her straight brown hair had a central parting and was firmly confined either side; she wore a white shirt with collar and tie under her tweed suit.

She walked round the corner of the house and held out a hand to Bella. "Well met!" she announced. "You don't know me, of course, but I know all about you, Miss Cloud, and I felt I must be one of the first to welcome you back to the old homestead as it were."

Bella put the mugs down and took the outstretched hand. "That's nice of you, but I'm not Miss Cloud but her cousin Bella Duncan. That's Ann there on the grass."

"Well! What do you know!" Their visitor was not obviously taken aback although, relaxed and happy, playing with her pet, Ann looked like a girl of seventeen. Ann walked up the steps to shake the hand outstretched in her direction.

"I'm Janet Crane. I live at the other end of the village, last house before the hill. My father is the vet. I keep chickens, you've probably seen them out in the road, always getting out, blast them!" Bella gave Ann her coffee and offered to get one for their visitor.

"Not at this hour, thanks. Got a lot to do before I can expect my cuppa!" Ann and Bella sat on the top step with Miss Crane between them.

"Can't stop long – just wanted to enrol you both into my gang of helpers. I run the Guides, you know, and the WI. Both very worthwhile and we are terribly short of helpers. There is not much entertainment for youngsters round here so our Guide Company fills a real need and gives girls another interest apart from the inevitable boyfriend. As for the WI there are interesting lectures, craft demonstrations, cake stalls, coach trips and so on. Gives the wives a change from housework and looking after hubbie and kids. Such a boring kind of life! Then there are quite a fair number of activities in connection with the church. Can you sing? I sing in the choir, we could do with more voices. There is the MU, flower club, brasses, bell ringing, Sunday school, plenty to keep one busy."

Ann was trying to find a pause in the spate of words. She did not want to be 'kept busy'. Bella was storing up every inflection, every gesture; here was another fine character part!

Miss Crane continued "That's it then. I'm sure I can count you in. Can you do Guides and WI?"

Ann was aware of panic, but decided she was not going to be bullied. "I'm awfully sorry" – she began; and was immediately aware of hostility, and continued desperately "You see we are only here for a short while – a few weeks at the most. It is no use joining these things when we have to leave so soon."

"Really? Seems a pity when you've only just come. You're not going to live here then? What will happen to the house?"

"I suppose it will be sold ... if anyone will buy it." Said Ann desolately.

"What a shame! I can't think how you can bear to let it go. You could easily get it in order. But some people just don't like the country. Can't understand it myself! Sooner live here than London any day!" She heaved herself to her feet.

"I'd rather live in the country too," said Ann warmly "But I just can't afford it."

"Can't afford it ...?" repeated Miss Crane incredulously, for she, too, knew of the fortune left by old Mrs Cloud. "Well, of course, some people expect more than others, but thank God my tastes are simple. I can get by on a shoestring. Have to if it comes to that. Tempus fugit; I must toddle along. Glad to have met you. Sorry you can't help us. Cheery-bye; be seeing you about no doubt." With a backward wave she stumped away round the corner of the house.

"You know, they all seem to think you are really wealthy," reflected Bella. "Don't they know the old lady left all her money to Herbert? Are you sure there isn't any more coming to you from somewhere or other?"

"Well, you heard what they said. I was to have the house because it had been left to my father, but the only money was the land. The only to get money was by selling it all. So I have either got the money and no house or the house and no money."

They considered this in silence: then from the copper beech at the edge of the lawn a cuckoo called loudly three times and flew out across the field towards the brook.

"Oh! Look! I've never seen a cuckoo so close before. You know, Bella, it is worth everything just to be here. Let's not worry about the village but just enjoy ourselves."

Chapter Ten

The next few days were fine and sunny, ideal for making the most of their country holiday. They went out exploring on their bicycles; or relaxed in the environs of Cloud's End. To say relaxed could be misleading because Ann spent every available minute working in her garden while Bella enjoyed cosseting the house. She polished floors and furniture and rubbed the windows until they sparkled in the sunshine, she also enjoyed preparing appetizing meals.

Ann went round the borders clearing out the grass and weeds and revelling in the variety of plants that were sprouting in the cleared spaces. She donned a pair of leather gloves and took the secateurs out to the rose garden. After that she found a dead branch and started to clear the green weed and dead leaves off the surface of the pond. She had not realized what a messy job that would be. She took her shoes off and stood in the water gathering armfuls of dripping wet debris and throwing them onto the bank. Water ran down her arms and soaked the front of her shirt and her jeans. After a time she became aware that someone was watching her. Another visitor!

The lady was slender, dressed in a well-cut two-piece made in green linen. Her shoes shone with recent polishing and her fair hair was caught back with combs into a French pleat. She had obviously arrived in the estate-car which was standing by the front door.

"You must be Ann Cloud," she said. There was a smile in her eyes as she continued, "I was told there were two smart young ladies from London living at Cloud's End."

"Oh we always dress up when we go into the village. It gives us confidence. But, for a messy job like this I wear my old clothes." Ann bent to put her shoes on, and smiled at her visitor "Do please come in and meet Bella, my cousin, while I find some dry clothes."

"I am sorry I interrupted you. It is so frustrating to have to leave a job half finished."

The lady seemed very self confident yet spoke with an understanding smile.

"Don't worry! I was not being very successful. I think I need something better than this old branch. I hope you will join us for a cup of tea." The lady was obviously someone special. Ann wondered who she was but did not quite like to ask. Her visitor realized her dilemma.

"I must introduce myself. I am Lady Kate Mallow Hampton from Mallow Hampton Castle. Your father was a bit older than my sons. We saw quite a lot of him at one time. He was very lonely after his father died."

Ann's face caught alight, as it always did when people spoke of her father. Lady Kate realized that there was more to her than first appearances had suggested.

"Dad told me so much about the house and the countryside but he never mentioned the people much," she said almost apologetically as they went in through the front door. Bella was coming in from the terrace, "Is that you Ann? I am just going to put the kettle on for tea."

Ann introduced her, "Meet Isobel Duncan, my cousin. And Bella! This is Lady Kate Mallow Hampton come to pay us a visit!"

Bella gave a gasp, "Oh my goodness! The gentry calling with us in our working clothes! – do go and change Ann – and nothing to eat for tea – not even cucumber sandwiches!" Ann disappeared to get changed while Bella escorted their visitor into the drawing room and went to put the kettle on.

Lady Kate eyed the few pieces of lovely furniture and the Aubusson carpet grouped together in the otherwise empty room with its fine proportions but stained wallpaper. Why do they not have curtains? She wondered. There must be some reason. Her son, David, had suggested she call but he couldn't have realized the apparent poverty of the place. However she was glad to have made the acquaintance of Humphrey's daughter who seemed a quiet girl with not much about her.

Bella came in with the tea tray. Ann followed with a plate of thin bread and butter. Quite adequate, thought Lady Kate and was pleased that the girl felt no compulsion to apologize for the meagre fare.

They had just begun their tea when a strange female figure was seen striding past the long windows and then a shrill voice was heard calling in the hall, "Anyone at home?"

Ann got up rather uncertainly. "How odd! Is it a special day for calling or something?"

"Do bring her in!" implored Lady Kate, "Whoever it is do bring her in!"

A large and oddly dressed young woman was standing in the hall. She wore a white tennis skirt of some substantial material which flared out in rigid folds, and above it a dark blue blazer with a club crest on the pocket. On her head was a panama hat with a club ribbon round it.

In one hand she bore a large gaily coloured golf umbrella. She advanced on Ann with outstretched hand.

"Good afternoon. May I introduce myself? Miss Claribel Gasper-Fugg, of the local Women's Institute, you know. I must persuade you to join us. May I leave my umbrella here?" And she planted her outsize brolly firmly in Mrs Nebworth's stand.

Ann began to giggle. It was quite impossible! It just could not be true! But it was! What was Lady Kate going to say?

"Have you got visitors?" hissed the newcomer. "Never mind! Take me in and introduce me!" Ann found herself being pushed through the door into the drawing room.

"This is M-miss M-mirabel Gasper-F-fugg about the Woman's Institute ..." began Ann in a quavering voice.

"Indeed!" Lady Kate regarded the newcomer with interest. "Our Woman's Institute? I don't think I ..."

At this point Bella took over.

"May I introduce a friend of ours, Lady Kate? This is Mr Adrian Peel."

Adrian took off the panama and bowed. "How did you guess?" he asked. The girls were too overcome with laughter to answer. He turned to Lady Kate. "You didn't guess, did you?" he asked.

"Not a clue," she assured him. "Except that I happen to know the woman who runs the local WI – Oh, so she has been to see you?" as the girls exclaimed – "So I had a suspicion something was odd. Do tell me, where did you get that wonderful costume?"

"Believe it or not, it's real. My Aunt Stella wore it when she used to play croquet at Ranelagh or Roehampton in the gay twenties. Fantastic isn't it?"

"You're quite right!" exclaimed Lady Kate, pursuing a thought of her own. "I remember seeing them wearing very similar clothes for the All England matches somewhere, when we went to watch the polo."

"Polo? You should not waste your time watching a gentle game like polo! For sheer venom, spite, and malice you watch croquet!"

"My dear boy, I think you must be a little prejudiced!" commented Lady Kate judicially, and the girls dissolved into fresh laughter.

A clatter on the terrace made them look up. They saw a man in breeches and a tweed jacket standing holding his horse outside the glass doors.

"That's my son, David Mallow Hampton," said Lady Kate. "He said he might ride over."

Ann went to the door and recognized the fair-haired man who had greeted her at church.

"Will you come in and have some tea?" she asked.

"Yes please. But first I must leave my mare somewhere. Do you mind if I take her onto your hayfield down there?"

"That's not a hayfield. It's the croquet lawn!"

"Croquet lawn! You could have fooled me," he muttered.

"Oh, I know it wants cutting but we have not got a mower." They walked down the slope at the end of the terrace. "It won't eat my flowers, will it?" Ann asked anxiously.

"Can I borrow that fork? I can secure her in the middle where she can't reach them."

They walked up the steps and into the house. Ann made introductions. "This is Lord Mallow Hampton; meet Bella Duncan, my cousin, and Adrian Peel." They shook hands and Bella left the room saying, "More cups and more tea! I'm afraid we can't offer you anything stronger."

Ann saw Lord David eyeing Adrian's outfit and started to giggle again, "Oh Adrian! Do and get changed while I explain." Assisted by Lady Kate, Ann managed to convince Lord David that Adrian was really quite sane. Then Ann continued, "He works for his uncle's legal firm, Merryweather, Nebworth and Merryweather. As they are London based Mr Herbert Cloud gave them the job of finding me because I inherit this house which was left to my father."

"I see." Lady Kate realized the attraction that two lively girls would have for a young man but did not comment. "And have you met your uncle?"

"No. He wrote to me soon after I got here and invited me to stay at his house, but I did not want to stay with strangers and Bella and I are very happy here on our own."

"It would not have hurt him to call and see how you were getting on."

"Oh please don't suggest it. He and his mother were not at all kind to my father."

"Has Mary Heriot been to call?" asked Lord David. "The vicar was most concerned when I told him you had been in church to hear his sermon about welcoming 'Angels Unaware'".

"Yes, she was really nice and made us feel we had at least one friend in the village."

"Only one! Who else have you met?"

"Well there is Mrs Quickly, who will only sell us bread if we put our money on the counter first," said Bella, "and Mr Sprite, the butcher, who promised to call but has never been near."

"And Janet Crane who was most put out because we would not help her with the WI," added Ann, beginning to giggle again as she looked at Adrian, who had returned to the room in his normal clothes.

"Don't forget the 'angry farmer'," put in Bella.

"'Angry farmer'?" echoed Lady Kate, "Who could that be?"

"He rents my fields, and when he saw me walking on them he shouted at me and told me to get off and keep off – Which I am certainly not going to do."

"That's Richard Brent from Shallowford farm," said Lord David. "I think he has had some unfortunate experiences lately with gates left open and cows lamed by broken glass. The main road runs through his land. It is easy to stop for a picnic."

"What a pity he made a bad start," said Lady Kate. "He is really a very nice lad and a bit lonely. I am sure he would like to be friends if you give him a chance."

"Can you tell us about Nellie Crouch?" Bella stood up, put the tea cosy on her head and did her 'character act'. "I can come and do yer floors for yer. Always did the old lady's, come at seven while she was still in bed. I'm a good worker I am, not like those lazy good-fer-nothing madams from the village." Adrian had not met Nellie Crouch and stared in surprise as Bella continued to recall her impressions of their first visitor. Lady Kate was overcome with helpless laughter and impressed by the skill with which Bella brought the character to life. "Yes, that's Nellie Crouch. I don't think you need to worry if she is not friendly."

"I think she really wanted to work here," said Ann sadly. "But we don't need anyone the short time we are here and anyway we can't afford to pay for help."

Lady Kate noted "short time" and "can't afford" but, before she could make tactful enquiries Ann jumped up and ran to pick up her kitten, which had just come through the door. "We think that Nellie Crouch left this for us. Isn't he sweet, so soft and cuddly. I have never had a pet before. I call him Caesar, Veni, Vidi, Vinci – he came, he saw, he conquered."

"Are you a Latin scholar?" asked Lord David.

"Not really. My father taught me a little but it is seven years since he died so I have forgotten most of it."

"I remember him reading Classics at Oxford," said Lady Kate.

"He enjoyed his time at Oxford," said Ann, "especially performing in the Shakespeare plays put on by the OUDS. That's where he met my mother, playing Bassanio to her Portia in *The Merchant of Venice*."

"I met her once," said Lady Kate. "She was a lively girl and," turning to Bella, "you remind me of her a little."

"She was my mother's sister," explained Bella.

"Of course. Well, it has been nice meeting you. Perhaps you would like to pay us a visit at Mallow Hampton Castle."

It sounded very grand. The girls were hesitant. "Well, yes, sometime when we are out on our bikes," said Bella. Lord David was more pressing with his invitation.

"Of course you must come," and, turning to Ann, "If you like animals you may like to see a foal I have got. It is just a week old."

"How gorgeous," breathed Ann. "Yes please."

"Right. Let's fix a day and I will come and fetch you."

Lady Kate followed that invitation with the comment, "You'd better tell them they may be travelling with a strong smell of pig! I'm used to farm animals but it is only fair to warn any guests that our farm transport is strictly utilitarian." A day was fixed for the following week. Ann went out with Lord David to release his horse, while Bella escorted Lady Kate out to her car.

As she drove off Lady Kate could not help wondering if she really wanted to get involved with two London girls, would they be inclined to take liberties?

Lord David was pleased to find two pretty girls to add to the social life in the area. That lively one, Bella, could be great fun to know.

Ann and Bella shut the front door and stood in the hall looking at each other.

"It's a red letter day!" said Bella "The gentry have called."

"Do you think Lady Kate really wants us to go?" said Ann "Mallow Hampton Castle sounds awfully grand."

"Let's just go this once and see how we get on. But I tell you one thing, we will make sure we are properly dressed. I never saw you looking such a mess, Ann, as when you came in all dripping wet!"

Adrian had joined them in the hall, "You'll be all right. Just be natural – but, perhaps you'd better not put on another of your Music Hall acts, Bella. Who was it? She seemed quite a character, and Lady Kate certainly knew her."

Ann started to giggle, "What about your Music Hall turn, Adrian? That caused quite a sensation!" Bella explained about Nellie Crouch, and they entertained Adrian with descriptions of their other visitors. "You may be out in the country but there seems to be plenty going on" was his comment as he left for home.

Chapter Eleven

The following week Ann and Bella gave some thought to their attire for the visit to Mallow Hampton castle.

"Let's hope it's fine and warm so that we can wear our new cotton dresses," said Ann. They went to the wardrobe, took the dresses out and hung them up to examine them.

"Yes, these will do nicely," said Bella. "But they are very creased and need ironing."

"We've not got an iron or an ironing board," said Ann. "I know what we can do. Let's go and call on the vicar's wife. She invited us, remember, and I am sure she would let us use her iron."

Mary Heriot was delighted to see them. "You're just in time for a cup of tea," she said. As they sat round the kitchen table Bella told her about their invitation to the castle.

"How nice that you have met Lady Kate. She has had a sad life; her husband was killed at the end of the First War and then, in 1940, both Lord David and his elder brother, Lord James, were called up. Lady Kate was left with the job of running the farm and the stables. I don't know how she kept going; and, then to crown it all, Lord James was killed just after the D Day landings in Normandy."

"How very sad," said Ann, her eyes filling with tears, while Bella's reaction was more robust. "At least Lord David came through all right."

"Yes. He and his mother are very close. He is very fond of her. I doubt if he will ever marry. It would have to be a very special kind of girl to fit in."

There was a short silence, which Bella broke. "I hope you won't mind, but the real reason we have come is to ask if you have an iron we could use. We must look presentable and our summer frocks are a bit creased."

Ann started to giggle. "When Lady Kate came we were both in our old clothes and I had been trying to clear the weed off the pond and was dripping wet."

"Yes, Ann looked a real ragamuffin," added Bella.

"So, you see, we want to make a good impression."

Mary Heriot was sympathetic and they continued to chat while Ann and Bella ironed the dresses and carefully folded them ready to be carried back to Cloud's End.

"While you are here you must see my studio." And Mary Heriot took them up to the large north-facing room, which contained an array of paints, brushes and other painting equipment. This meant little to the girls, neither of whom knew much about painting, but there were several oil paintings, views of the countryside, in bright clear colours that caught Ann's eye.

"These are lovely. When I have to go back to London I should want a picture like one of those on my wall to remind me of Cloud's End."

"Why do you have to go back to London?"

"I'm living on my savings and the rent from the fields. When that runs out I shall have to get a job."

"But we always thought that Mrs Cloud was very wealthy."

"She left all her money to my uncle. I only get the house because my grandfather left it to my father."

"That explains a lot," said Mary Heriot thoughtfully. "What kind of job have you been doing?"

"I trained as a shorthand typist and went to work in an office."

'There must be office jobs going in Mallow Greatham; or, perhaps you could get some kind of gardening job."

"That would be lovely, but where should I live? I don't really want to go on camping out alone in that big house."

"Oh Ann! Don't start worrying about jobs yet. You will have at least four more weeks and then you know you are very welcome to come back and live with Mum and me the same as you always have done." Bella's rough comment hid her concern for her young cousin.

"Yes, you're right. I must just enjoy life in the country while I am here."

When Lord David arrived the following day he found two smart young ladies waiting for him. Their hair had been washed and set and was held in place with spray. Bella's dress was the fashionable "New Look" with flared, calf length, skirt, in a bright angular pattern in different shades of green on a cream background. Ann's dress was more subdued and had a flowery design in shades of grey, blue and violet. Their faces had a healthy glow from their life in the open air so needed little make-up, but Bella said she felt naked without mascara and eye shadow.

Mallow Hampton Castle was found to be an imposing mansion built of stone. The girls were too polite to comment but Lord David explained, "One of my great grandfathers about 150 years ago married an heiress. He fancied a stone house so imported craftsmen and materials from the next county – not too far away. The porch is rather large," he added as he ushered them in. "There is a chapel built over it."

He took them into the drawing room where Lady Kate was waiting. Bella went to shake hands with her while Ann stood just inside the door and looked at the room. It was about the same size as that at Cloud's End but – oh how different! The walls and paint were bright and clean; there were long velvet curtains at the windows, a grand piano and glass-fronted cabinets with fine china. Comfortable chairs were grouped round the fireplace with small elegant tables handy to hold tea cups or wine glasses.

"What a lovely room," she breathed. "I'm sure Cloud's End looked like this when my father lived there."

"Well you've got some nice furniture. Why don't you get the rest out of store and have the room decorated?"

"The furniture is on loan from Mrs Nebworth, Adrian's aunt. It's not mine. I never thought about there being any in store, would that be mine?"

"I'm not sure, you would have to ask Herbert Cloud but I can't imagine him giving nice furniture away."

"It does not really matter. I can't afford to have the house repainted. Once my savings are used up I shall have to go back to London and find a job."

"But old Mrs Cloud was a very wealthy woman; it cannot all have gone in Death Duties."

"Oh no! She left all the money to my uncle. I only get the house because my grandfather left it to my father. I shall have to sell it. I'm just enjoying my holiday camping out for a few weeks."

"I expect you will be pleased to get back to London."

"No, I shall be miserable without my garden. I have been spending every possible minute out there. It's wonderful to see the spring flowers coming into bloom." As she said this she came to shake hands and sit down. An elderly woman in a check overall came into the room wheeling a trolley.

"Here is Harriet with the tea," said Lady Kate. "Harriet this is Miss Ann Cloud, Mr Humphrey's daughter."

Ann stood up and went to shake hands. "Did you know my father?"

"Indeed I did! When he was young he was mad on horses and spent all his spare time in the stables. He had a special set of working clothes he kept here. Mrs Cloud could not bear the smell of horses."

"He never had a chance to ride in London; he had to teach to earn his living."

"Do you like horses?" asked Lord David as Harriet left the room.

"Next time you come you must bring slacks and then you can have a ride."

"I like most animals but I have always found horses a bit big," said Ann.

Lord David turned to Bella, "How about you Miss Duncan? Would you like to ride?"

Bella was not sure. "I'm not really a sporty type," she said. "I expect riding needs a lot of practice and I'm likely to spend most of my time in London."

"Do I gather that you are an actress like Ann's mother?" asked Lady Kate.

"Yes, and she had a great success playing Rosalind in *As You Like It* last year," said Ann proudly.

"Ought we to have seen you?" asked Lady Kate. "Living out here we don't often get into town to see the shows. In fact during the war I got out of the habit. It was not really possible; I was working flat out keeping things running here while James and David were soldiering."

"Rosalind was the best part I have had to date," said Bella. "But I keep hoping. In fact I shall have to go back soon for a few days to audition for a play for the BBC."

"I've had an idea," said Lord David. "We need someone special to open our Garden Fete in June. How about it Miss Duncan?"

"Well, I don't know that I am that special. Is it a very grand affair?"

"It is partly social and partly to raise money for village activities; the church, the WI, Girl Guides, Flower Club and so on. Each group has a stall and we have side shows like bowling for the pig, pony rides for the children, fancy dress competition and country dancing," said Lady Kate.

"And the Brass Band from Mallow Greatham to rouse the neighbourhood," added Lord David. "Think about it. It would be nice to have someone completely different."

"Well I don't know!" Ann could sense that Bella was visualizing herself as the 'well known actress'. "I have the impression that the opener has to go round patronizing all the stalls. I am afraid I would not be able to be very generous."

"Most of the sideshows only charge tuppence or threepence a go," said Lord David. "It just needs someone to enjoy themselves and encourage others to join in."

"Maybe I could get Adrian Peel to come along as my 'escort'."

'Adrian Peel? – Oh, the lad in the croquet kit! I expect he would enjoy it."

Lady Kate was less enthusiastic. "I don't think the village would be very impressed if they found out that the Special Guest to open the Fete was one of the two girls who had been camping out at Cloud's End."

Lord David decided to change the subject. "We saw Richard Brent busy earthing up his potatoes as we came along," he said. "I know there is a lot to do on the farm but, surely, he can take Saturday afternoon off. That farm is an obsession with him."

"And you know the reason why," said Lady Kate.

"Was there some tragedy?" asked Bella.

"Yes – it happened during the war when we had to grow as much food as possible ... or impossible! The government set up a body composed, often, of the most extraordinary people, who knew nothing about farming and had the most outrageous powers, to tell farmers how to run their farms. He came to me. I was struggling with James and David away in the army but I was not having interference and told him so in no uncertain terms."

"I bet you did!" interjected Lord David.

"Poor Mr Brent had had a couple of bad seasons so this official told him the land was not being properly farmed and must be handed over to someone else. It was quite inexcusable! ... Walter Brent was in a bad way. His wife had died recently, Richard was away at school, he was ill and overworked and had no-one to discuss it with ... and, whether it was an accident or not, nobody knows, but he was found out in the fields one morning with his gun beside him."

"Oh, how tragic!" Ann's face went white, and both girls looked so distressed that Lord David continued hastily. "So you can understand why Richard feels he has to fight to keep his end up. He may be a bit crusty on occasion but he is all right underneath ... No point in worrying about things you can't change ... Now you have finished your tea perhaps you would like to come out and see the stables."

"Can we see the foal you told us about?" asked Ann.

They spent a happy hour. Lord David showed them how to offer sugar or an apple to the horses on the palm of the hand, Ann was thrilled by the sight of the foal and its mother. They both left feeling it had been a memorable day. Bella felt her experience of the 'country house' atmosphere could be helpful for future parts; while Ann had much to consider. How could her father have seemed so contented when forced to live such a different life? And would understanding the problems of her "angry farmer" help her to be more friendly and make allowances for his abrupt manner when, as was inevitable in a village, she met him again?

Chapter Twelve

The warm sunny spell came to an end. Richard Brent knocked on the front door of Cloud's End on a chilly damp morning. As nobody came to answer it he walked in carrying two bottles of milk. "Anyone there?" he called. An indistinct reply, drowned by a bout of coughing came from one of the rooms. He put the milk down on the table and opened the door on the left. Once inside he stood staring. In Mrs Cloud's time the room had been full of handsome furniture and the windows curtained with velvet. Now he looked past the few items in the centre of the room to the girl lying on the settee wrapped in blankets and coughing.

"Are you all right?" he asked.

"I think I've got the 'flu," said Ann.

"Could be! There's a lot going round. Tom Hoby has got it so I have brought the milk. Are you on your own? Where is your friend?" He came in and stood looking down at her.

"Bella has gone to London. " Ann looked up at the tall young man, his dark hair plastered down by the rain and a look of astonishment on his face. He's not much older than me, she thought and started to cough again.

Something obviously had to be done but first things first. "Can I get you a hot drink?" he asked. Still coughing she nodded. Then, as he turned to go,

"And please ..."

"Well?"

"Could you let Caesar out."

"Caesar?"

"My kitten, I shut him in the back kitchen when I fed him this morning."

Richard set off to explore. He looked in through the door across the hall and saw the two camp beds; then went through the door by the stairs and found the kitchen. He filled the kettle and set it on the stove. While it boiled he went to look for the kitten. It jumped out of its box, he picked it up and went back to Ann.

"What do you want me to do with him?" he asked.

"Give him to me please."

While he set the tray and searched for milk, sugar and biscuits his brain was busy. How long was the girl going to be alone in this big empty house? Who was going to look after her? What should he do about it? He would need to make some tactful enquiries, and tact was not his strong point!

So, when Ann had been provided with a mug of steaming hot tea, he pulled up a chair, sat down and picked up his own mug.

"You don't look very comfortable there. You ought to be in bed."

"It's better than the camp bed, and my cough is worse when I'm lying flat."

"How long has your friend been away?"

"She went early yesterday morning. I was all right then."

"Or said you were! When is she coming back?"

"She has gone to see about a new contract. We are coming to the end of our holiday."

"Holiday?"

"Yes, camping out here in the house where my father grew up before it is sold."

"Sold?"

"Yes, there's no money. I can't afford to live here."

"But we all thought Mrs Cloud was so wealthy."

"She left all her money to my uncle Herbert."

"So?"

"I either have the house and no money or money and no house." Ann put her hands over her face to hide the tears. It was all too much ... miserable weather, feeling ill and the thought of having to leave her beloved garden.

"It can't be as bad as all that." Faced for the first time in his life with someone else's problems Richard felt he had to take action.

"The first thing we must do is to arrange for you to be looked after; I don't think the hospital would take you and I doubt if a nurse would enjoy 'camping out' much, so, I think the only thing is for you to come to Shallowford farm where my old nannie, Mrs Bunch, can cosset you. She would really enjoy that. I'm never ill."

The thought of being "cosseted" was very appealing but Ann felt she had to protest. "Oh no, I don't want to be a trouble to any one. I shall be quite all right." And she began to cough again.

"You know you've really got no choice. If you won't come willingly I shall have to kidnap you. Do say you'll come."

Ann smiled weakly, "Yes please."

"Good girl," he patted her hand. "Now I will go and tell Nannie

Bunch to get a bed ready with plenty of hot water bottles, and be back to collect you in about an hour. Do you think you will be able to pack what you will need, or shall I bring her back to do it for you?"

"No, I can do that."

Off he went leaving Ann with the thought of subsiding into a warm comfy bed over-riding all other considerations.

True to his word he was back in an hour and ran into a snag.

"I can't leave Caesar," said Ann. "Will it be all right if I bring him?"

"There are other cats and dogs at the farm. You must not mind if they attack him. I would offer to come here and feed him but I have not really got time with all the jobs on the farm."

"If you don't mind I would like to bring him. He is special, my very first pet."

So Ann carried Caesar into the land-rover and he was safely imprisoned under the blanket that Richard tucked round her.

The drive down the hill, the welcome by Mrs Bunch and the climb up the narrow stairs all seemed like a dream to Ann as she snuggled down into the soft warm bed. She was woken by Mrs Bunch.

"I've brought you some soup my dear. I made it myself with fresh vegetables. You do look peaky. I'll need to feed you up."

After the evening meal Richard came into the room.

"I think your friend ought to know where you are in case she comes back and finds the house empty."

"She is my cousin, Bella Duncan. Maybe I will have the energy to write her a note tomorrow."

"Don't worry. If you give me her address I will drop her a line and post it in the morning."

"Oh thank you. You are so kind."

As he went out and closed the door Richard wondered what had led him to befriend this rather uninteresting girl. But he really had no choice, his life with animals had conditioned him to rescue and look after all sick creatures. Anyway, with Nannie Bunch to look after her and feed her up in a few days she would be well enough to go back to Cloud's End and he would be rid of her.

While Ann was in bed Mrs Bunch was in and out of her room, sharing cups of tea and chatting. She heard all about the legacy and the girls' camping adventures. A sympathetic ear invites confidences and she soon became very much aware of Ann's enjoyment of the countryside and the garden.

"How can I bear to go back to London and leave my garden behind?" asked Ann.

That was a problem Mrs Bunch discussed with Richard as they ate their tea.

"Do we have to let her go back to town and be miserable away from the country?" she asked. "Surely she can find a job here working on a farm or in a garden."

"I can see you will be busy on her behalf but she will need somewhere to live you know, she can't stay here and she has to sell the house." Richard was a bit damping. He had done his share, let Mrs Bunch get involved if she felt like it.

Ann's bedroom window looked out over the farmyard. Even with the window closed she could hear the sounds of constant activity. Very often Richard's voice could be heard shouting, "Get a move on! Don't take all day!" Do the men mind being shouted at, she wondered.

On the third day Ann decided to get up. Mrs Bunch was glad to see that her patient was feeling better.

It will do you good to come down for a bit. I will light the fire in the parlour and tell Mr Richard to finish early so that he can come and have a cup of tea with you," she said.

"Oh please! I don't want to be a bother."

"It will be good for him to take an hour off. He works much too hard and I can't stop him."

"Is it because of his father?" asked Ann a little hesitantly.

"You have heard about that have you? Yes. The farm got very run down and I think he feels he has to make a success of it or die in the attempt. That girl he got engaged to did not help him either. She was quite the wrong sort and did not try to understand him."

Ann felt a bit apprehensive about this tea party but, settled down in front of the fire with a book, became so absorbed in the adventure story that she did not realize Richard had come in until he was standing in front of her asking if she was feeling better.

"Oh!" she gasped. "Yes thank you, and I have to thank you for rescuing me. I am very grateful."

It was his turn to be embarrassed. "Don't mention it. Nothing else I could do." And, to change the subject, "I see you have a good book."

"Yes," she held it up to show him. "Mrs Bunch found it for me. It is *The Three Hostages* by John Buchan."

"Is it the first time you have read it? It is one of my favourites." And they settled down to animated discussion about the books they had read and enjoyed. Both were surprised how quickly and pleasantly the time had gone when Mrs Bunch came in to tell Ann she should go back to bed.

"It has gone six, you've been up quite long enough for your first day."

"I don't feel tired at all," protested Ann but, once undressed, found she was glad to get back into bed.

The next day she was allowed to get up after breakfast. Mrs Bunch put a chair in a sunny corner of the garden.

"There you are," she said. "Wrap up warm. It will do you good to sit outside for a bit."

Ann sat back in the chair and looked about her. It was only a small garden but, obviously, there was no-one with time to look after it. The grass had been cut but the flower beds that bordered the lawn on three sides were badly in need of weeding. It only needed the sight of a small hand fork standing against the wall to get Ann out of her chair and onto her knees. By the time Mrs Bunch came out to tell her that lunch was ready she had made quite an impact on the first of the three sides.

"Oh my goodness!" exclaimed Mrs Bunch. "You're not supposed to be doing that!"

Ann turned a scared face towards her. "Will he mind? Should I have asked if I could? But the garden looked so neglected."

"Mr Richard won't mind. He never bothers with the garden. It's you I was thinking about, you don't want to tire yourself out."

Ann stood up a bit shakily. "Yes, perhaps I better rest on my bed this afternoon. I'll have another go tomorrow."

Next morning she was having breakfast with Mrs Bunch and Richard when the post arrived. There was a letter for her from Bella. As she opened it she was startled by an exclamation from Richard.

"Blasted bureaucrats!"

"What's the matter?" she asked.

"They want to know why I have not sent in my 'pig form'!"

"Pig form?"

"Yes, it is a long document wanting details of colour, shape and size of all the pigs on the farm. I never have had pigs and never will! It's a complete waste of time! It's not only pigs, it is cows and sheep and hens and wheat and oats and barley and anything else they can think of! I've got a pile of forms and never get time to deal with them."

"Could I help?" asked Ann. "Working in an office I did a lot of form filling. Perhaps I could deal with them for you." Richard went to his desk and dumped an untidy pile of papers on the table in front of her.

"You can have a look through these if you like," he said. "I doubt whether you will be able to make much of them."

Ann spent the morning sorting through the jungle. She clipped together those for each farm product. It seemed the government had an insatiable appetite for statistics. She was concerned at the number of reminders with financial penalties for failure to comply. By the time Richard came in for his lunch she had a list to discuss with him.

"There must be some of these that don't apply. Tell me which and I will send in nil returns. Then, maybe, we can work through the others this evening." Richard was surprised to find the girl so businesslike and organized.

"Also, I have found these letters mixed up with the forms. I can take down your replies in shorthand and type them for you. Have you got a typewriter?"

"No, and I don't know who would have one."

"Can't you try to find one?"

"Maybe Lady Kate would have one. She employed a secretary during the war."

"Can you ring her up and find out? Do it now!"

Wretched girl! She was pushing him into action. "There's not really all that hurry!" But he picked up the phone. "Mallow Hampton Castle? Hello David. Can you tell me, have you got a typewriter? ... Could I borrow it for a few days please? ... No. I can't type; I've got a temporary secretary ... I'll be round to collect it at the week-end ... Will you really? Tomorrow morning? Come to coffee. See you!"

He put the phone down and turned to Ann.

"He says he scents a mystery and he can't wait to find out. Inquisitive beggar!"

Ann was starting to giggle. "Do you want me to hide?"

"No of course not! You can do the explaining."

As they were drinking their coffee the following morning there was a bang on the door and Lord David marched in and put the typewriter he was carrying on the table.

"Hello there Ricky my boy! I have come to see if you are entertaining 'Angels Unaware'?" He turned to Ann. "Well met Miss Cloud. I thought you might be here."

Ann explained about the flu and the letters. "You see, I am a trained secretary and have offered to get Richard up-to-date with his correspondence."

"If you do that it will be the first time ever ... and there are some others of us who need help. How about coming to the Castle and looking at my pile of papers?"

"I thought your mother took care of your paperwork," said Richard.

"Yes, but she does not really enjoy it. When it gets on top of her Janet Crane comes in to give a hand."

"Janet Crane! Is she the vet's daughter?" asked Ann. "She was fed up with us because we would not help with the Guides. I thought she seemed very bossy."

"She seems to spend all her time running the village and there is not really all that much to do," commented Lord David.

"I seem to remember her winning all the prizes at pony club meets before the war," said Richard. "Does she still ride?"

"No, she says she is too busy helping her father; but, now he is getting a young assistant, things should be easier. Which reminds me, I have got Mr Crane coming to look at one of my horses so must get back before he comes. Goodbye Miss Cloud, see you before too long I expect."

As she started to type Richard's letters Ann was wondering if all farmers had the same paperwork problem and would they be prepared to pay for secretarial help? Could she make a living that way? Could she find somewhere to live? She could not live alone at Cloud's End, it was too big and lonely.

Chapter Thirteen

Janet Crane was talking to Lord David standing outside Mallow Greening vicarage in the morning sunshine. " ... and it is the WI outing on Saturday. We're going to London for the day. There are some spare seats on the coach. Can I sell you a ticket?"

"Oh no! Not my kind of thing at all! Please excuse me. I want a word with Miss Duncan. I've just seen her go into Jolly's shop." And he walked off with a brief lift of his cap.

Janet Crane was shaken by his sudden departure. Tears sprung into her eyes. She turned to find Mary Heriot standing beside her.

"Did you see that? Just walked off and left me! He would never have done that before those two girls came to Cloud's End."

"Maybe he's just being friendly to strangers," said Mary Heriot. "Come in and tell me about the WI outing. I was just going to make a cup of coffee."

There was a large mirror in the vicarage hall. Janet stood and regarded her reflection. "Do you think David would like me better if I had fair hair and blue eyes?" she asked.

"No; but you don't take much trouble with your appearance do you?" said Mary as she put the kettle on the stove.

"I stopped bothering after Patrick was killed."

"I know! It was sad for you losing your fiancé like that, but that was six years ago and life has to go on."

"What do you think I should do?"

"When you go up to London on Saturday why don't you go to a really good hairdresser and change your hair-style?"

"I don't want a lot of curls. It would not be me."

Mary considered Janet's rather square face with her artist's eye. "I think you would look nicer with a side parting and have your hair cut shorter at the sides."

"I want to get some new clothes as well. Have you any ideas?"

"Now the summer is coming you could wear open-necked shirts. Collar and tie are a bit formal for every-day wear. Get coloured ones. Peach or honey colour would suit you, not blue or pink."

Janet considered this. "Yes! Perhaps you are right. There is something else I should like your advice on. You see; now that my Father has got this assistant I am not needed to help run the vet's business. I was talking to Jerry Jackson the other day when he came to collect supplies for his medicine cupboard. He runs this stable in Mallow Greatham and was saying how difficult he finds it to get good grooms and stable boys. I wondered if I should offer to go and help?"

"Why don't you buy a well-cut pair of jodhpurs and some cheaper ones for every-day use and give it a try? Do a good job and make sure you get paid for it."

"Paid?"

"Of course! You want Jerry to take you seriously don't you? Go and see him today."

"Yes! I might do that," said Janet starting to take off her tie.

Mary was pleased at this positive reaction. "How about coming up to the mirror in my room? I'm not a trained hair stylist but I've got a pair of thinning scissors. If I lighten the back and sides your hair will fall into a less formal shape."

Twenty minutes later Janet left the vicarage in a buoyant mood on her way to cycle into Mallow Greatham.

Lord David caught up with the girls as they entered Mr Jolly's shop.

"Good morning ladies! Can I interest you in tickets for the WI coach outing to London?"

"Oh, I don't think so, thank you."

"Janet Crane has been trying to get me to buy one. She seemed a bit desperate. I suppose it will make a loss. Never mind; we can always subsidize it from the proceeds of the Fete."

"Do you still want me to come and open it?" said Bella.

"Yes. I have talked my Mother round. Can we have a talk about it? Let me treat you to lunch at the White Hart in Mallow Greatham." The tall man standing at the counter turned round.

"Am I invited too?" asked Richard Brent.

"Of course; but you will have to find a tie and a jacket from somewhere. You know how particular they are."

"No problem! I must tell Mrs Bunch I shall not want lunch. Come with me Ann, she will like to see you." Ann hesitated and looked at Bella.

"Go with Richard. He'll like to have your company."

"Of course I will."

At the farm Ann took the opportunity to tidy her hair and repair her make-up. She was glad she had done so when she saw Richard running down the stairs in flannels, a clean shirt, jacket and tie.

In the White Hart car park the Land-rover pulled into a space alongside a bright yellow Aston Martin. Richard got out and stood looking gloomily at the sports car.

"Oh lordy! Look who's here!"

"What is the matter?"

"That car belongs to Julie. I was engaged to her before she decided to marry Warrener, and I have not seen her since. She'll be in the bar with the gang. Let's go in through the kitchen." He brushed a hand through his hair, destroying the careful brushing and looked miserable. "I suppose I shall have to meet her someday but I just feel I can't – yet!"

Ann was surprised at Richard's reaction. She had not thought him to be so sensitive. He must have been badly hurt.

"Does it matter as much as all that?" she queried. "Can't you shrug it off and not care? Or do you care? Are you still in love with her?"

"No, thank God! But it still hurts – mostly to think I was such a fool."

"Well why not show her you no longer care? You're bound to meet her one day. This is as good a place as any, the longer you put it off the worse it will get."

It was the kind of advice he had often been tempted to give to her, as he recognized with a reluctant grin.

"Wise girl! ... All right! I'll have a go. Back me up won't you." He marched up to the door, held it open and ushered Ann into the bar lounge. She had no idea what was going to happen and must have looked as vacant as she felt being confronted with a chattering group, who did not know her nor she them.

The youngest of the three women caught sight of Richard.

"Look who's here!" she cried, lifting her glass to them. "Do come and drink with us Ricky-Dick!"

"Good Lord!" exclaimed Richard in well simulated surprise, "Who would have thought to find you here? Ann, I must introduce you to an old friend ... Julia – Mrs Warrener isn't it? Ann Cloud."

The introduction was acknowledged with a cool "How nice to meet you" as Julia flashed her eyelashes at Richard. "Come and meet everybody, especially this type in the natty suiting. Wally darling this is my ex!" Richard moved into the group and shook hands with the man with the flamboyant tie.

"Pleased to meet you," he said. "Which of you should I congratulate?" and, realizing that was not exactly tactful hastened to add "Congratulations to you both of course!" Julia put up a hand to push her long, silky, ash blonde hair away from her face. He remembered that gesture but did not think her hair had been quite that pale.

"Thank you Richard. We're having a great time, aren't we Wally?"

"Of course, my dear!" The man was obviously infatuated!

Ann stood watching. It was easy to see that Julia did not mean to let him escape too soon. As she watched a voice spoke at her elbow. "Let me get you a drink Miss Cloud. What will you have? Sherry, Martini, whisky-soda?"

She had no idea who he was. Tall and thin with a pair of very shrewd grey eyes. She chose the least exotic alternative. "Sherry please."

As he handed her the glass he introduced himself. "My name's Jackson. I run a stable here in Mallow Greatham. I don't suppose you ride."

Ann shook her head. "No I've never had the opportunity, but Lord David has promised to teach me."

"Oh, am I right in thinking you are the 'Missing Heiress'?"

Ann was aware of a hush in the conversation as they waited for her answer.

"I shouldn't think so," she replied. "I'm certainly not an heiress and I don't think I'm missing." She had no intention of being funny but several people laughed.

"You are not related to Herbert Cloud then?"

"Yes, I believe he is my uncle."

"Then you are the missing heiress." He said, smiling at her with a friendliness that prevented her from snubbing him further. "My dear girl, it was all over the town when you were found. Why, it's romance in capital letters!"

"I don't see why," she answered flatly. "There was nothing extraordinary about it. I was there all the time if they had bothered to look."

"Not quite as simple as that was it? I believe I'm right in saying ..."

But Ann had had enough of it. "Do forgive me, but we are meeting friends for lunch and we simply must go. Look at the time, Richard. We will be terribly late!" She went over to Richard and put a hand on his sleeve. He smiled down at her.

"Quite right! We must ask you all to excuse us and say goodbye."

They found Bella and Lord David waiting for them in the dining room.

"Whatever kept you?" asked Lord David.

"We thought you were never coming," added Bella.

"Julia was there with her new man," explained Richard. "I had to go and congratulate her."

"They were married six months ago. Haven't you seen her since?"

"Well – er – no – I've been too busy on the farm!"

"Oh – I see! Now there's no longer any need for you to shut yourself up on that farm of yours!" Richard frowned. David understood too much! He hastened to change the subject.

"What are we eating then?" he asked, as he picked up the menu.

An elderly man, who had been watching them, got up from his table and strode heavily across the room.

"Good morning Lord Mallow Hampton," he said. "Forgive me for interrupting your lunch, but may I speak to one of your guests? I believe I am correct in supposing this young lady to be my niece, Miss Anastasia Cloud." He spoke to Lord David but looked at Ann. She stared back at him, finding it difficult to believe that this was her father's brother. This man was only a pale replica of her father's vital good looks and vigorous energy.

"Yes, I am Anastasia Cloud," she answered gravely. Lord David got to his feet.

"May I introduce you? This is Miss Gordon, Mr Cloud. Mr Brent of course you know and," with a gentle smile – "As you rightly surmise, your niece! May I suggest you join us for coffee in the lounge after our meal, then you and Ann can talk more easily." To their relief he accepted the suggestion, nodded, and returned to his place.

Lord David laid a comforting hand over Ann's, "Eat up my girl. Don't let him spoil your lunch. You had to meet him sometime – just as well you were with friends!"

"Would you suppose his sudden friendliness was due to finding us in the exalted company of Lord Mallow Hampton?" enquired Richard darkly.

"Possibly! I must admit he is not one of my favourite people, but we all have to live and let live as best we can. You don't want to make an enemy of him, Ann."

"Well, he's not one of my favourite people either," she admitted. "How could he be? He never made any effort to get in touch with Dad, and it was only when my grandmother died and he had no alternative that he tried to find me. Even then, it was Adrian's firm that did the work not his – "

"Yes, but Adrian comes from a London firm. It is quite usual for a country firm to make use of an agent for London business."

Ann pondered this. "I have to remind myself that he is Dad's brother and I don't want to add to the bitterness; but I can't make myself feel friendly."

"I can understand that, but you may find you like him better than you think you will – or you may like the family – after all, relations do sometimes like each other!"

"In any case, you are bound to see him again," put in Richard forcibly.

"You don't suppose we're going to let you walk out of our lives and make no attempt to see you again, do you? I'm sure you feel the same as I do, David."

"Of course! So, you are sure to meet him, or his family, here and about in the years to come, and it will be much easier if you are on speaking terms."

Ann sat silent, she was feeling quite overwhelmed at this warm assurance that the end of their stay would not mean the end of these new friendships. Sensing her emotion, Bella spoke for her.

"That's a lovely thought, and very sweet of you both to make us feel that we belong here. Ann does, of course, through her family, but I'm a complete intruder. It occurs to me that perhaps I shouldn't be in on the next scene."

"Oh please!" exclaimed Ann. "You're much more my relation than Uncle Herbert is. I am not sure I really want to see him ... anyway you must come and support me."

"To be honest, I don't think I had better come," said Richard with a grin. "I can't bear the old blighter, and if he starts being rude to Ann, I shall feel inclined to dot him one!"

"In that case, it would definitely be wiser to leave you out. We want to play this very calmly. Don't wait for us. I'll bring the girls home."

Richard pulled a face. "OK boss, if you say so. Thanks for my lunch – And thanks to you, Ann for you know what. You never told me your name was Anastasia but I suppose I'll get used to it. Cheerio." And off he went.

They found a table in the lounge and ordered coffee. Herbert Cloud joined them. He was obviously determined to make a good impression.

"Forgive me for not getting in touch with you before this," he observed to Ann. "But I quite understood from your letter that you were only here for a short time and had thought you must have gone back to London long ago. Or, perhaps you are back on another visit?"

"Oh no! We have been here all the time," confessed Ann. "But it won't be for much longer, although I would like to make it last as long as possible." He glanced at her from beneath lowered lids. Bella wondered to herself if he realized that their stay was limited by shortness of funds.

Ann volunteered no more information, and, after a pause, he continued. "I hope you are enjoying your stay. I am afraid the house cannot be very comfortable. My wife and I were horrified to hear you were staying there. It has been empty for so long and needs so much doing to it."

"I know it does," agreed Ann. "But I particularly wanted to stay in the house that my father had told me so much about."

"Of course, of course, very understandable. I am sorry it is not in better order, but my mother refused to have anything done. Old people dislike the disturbance of workmen around. At the last she became very autocratic. You will remember her, my lord?"

"Yes, she always liked her own way," said Lord David equably.

Question answer. Question answer. There's nothing in the man thought Bella. Ann was never very conversational with strangers. Eventually Mr Cloud got round to asking them to meet his wife and family. Even then he hesitated, saying he would ask his wife which day would suit. Is she so bossy then? Wondered Bella.

"We would love to come sometime," Ann was more effusive than she felt. "Whenever it suits you. I can't very well ask you to visit us because we are only camping out. We have not much furniture. That reminds me, I have been meaning to ask what happened to the furniture that was in the house, or doesn't it come to me?"

Mr Cloud seemed a bit embarrassed. "I could not tell you about that without consulting my father's will. If I remember rightly, there was no definite instruction."

"I would have thought the furniture should go with the house," commented Lord David. "I suppose you can tell us what has happened to it."

"Well, you see, Emily, my daughter, was getting married and setting up house, so we were sure that her grandmother would have liked her to have the bedroom furniture, beds and linen. Not a lot of value in them but still in short supply after the war."

"And the lounge furniture and curtains? Lady Jane told me there were some nice things. Do you know what happened to them?"

"We did not quite know what to do and did not want to pay storage charges, so we have them stacked in the old coach house at the back of our offices."

"I should like to have a look to see what's there."

"Not very easy, I'm afraid. As they are at present you can hardly get inside the door."

"I am sure you will have taken care that none of the things has been damaged by rough handling or damp," said Lord David.

"Yes," said Ann. " And, if they are really mine I should like to see them sometime."

"Yes, of course, and we must have a business discussion one of these days," announced Mr Cloud. "You must tell me what you wish me to do about the house. Perhaps you would come to the office first and we can have our talk, and then we can go back to the house to have tea and meet the family."

Ann looked bewildered, "But isn't Adrian – I mean Mr Nebworth – doing everything like that for me?"

Mr Cloud pursed his lips. "Just as you like, of course, if you have already instructed him."

"Well, you see he was the only one I knew," pointed out Ann meekly. "They've done everything for me so far. It never occurred to me that anyone else would. Thank you very much all the same."

This seemed to bring them to a full stop. Lord David stood up.

"Sorry to cut the party short, but we must go girls, my mother will be waiting for us. I'm glad I was able to introduce you to your niece, Cloud. Odd that it should happen by chance after all this time."

"Yes indeed! It is quite an occasion! My children will be excited to hear about their new cousin! I sincerely hope you will soon be meeting them, my dear!"

Ann's eyes followed him as he left the room. Lord David grasped her hand and pulled her to her feet.

"Cheer up Ann! Before this happened you had an uncle you did not know – now you have one you don't like! It doesn't really matter all that much – now does it?" Ann smiled at him gratefully as she followed him out to the waiting estate car.

Chapter Fourteen

Ann and Bella were once again established at Cloud's End. Ann, spending every possible minute in the garden, had now progressed to the walled vegetable garden; while Bella, who did not really enjoy slaving out of doors, had established herself on a chair on the terrace and was concentrating on studying the part she had been given when in London. She looked up to see Ann standing in front of her.

"I think it must be coffee time," said Ann, "and look what I have found." She crushed the bunch of green leaves in her hand and held it out to Bella. "Smell! It is fresh mint. Just what we need to make mint sauce to go with our lamb!"

"But we are not having lamb – at least – "

"At least – what?

"I saw Adrian a couple of times while I was in London." Bella seemed a little embarrassed.

"That was nice!"

"And he plans to come and visit us on Saturday. We could cook lamb and mint sauce with green peas and potatoes and have a dinner party."

"Do you think Lord David would come as well?"

"No, I don't think we are smart enough for him. He is not the type to appreciate 'camping out'. Why don't you ask Richard? Adrian hasn't met him yet."

Ann considered this. "Yes, he is my tenant. It could be a good idea. Shall I go down to the farm and ask him?"

"Have your coffee first. You'd better leave it 'til he comes in for his lunch or you could have a job to find him."

Richard accepted with enthusiasm, and the girls went into the village to buy suitable provisions.

On Saturday morning as they were busy cleaning the hall floor and polishing the dining table a knock on the front door surprised them.

"I wonder who that can be," said Bella.

Ann opened the door to find two small boys standing there, their abandoned bicycles lying on the drive behind them.

"Hello!" said Ann.

"My name is Simon Cloud," said the fair boy. "Is one of you my cousin?"

"I am!" Ann beamed at him. "I'm Ann Cloud, and this is Bella Gordon. How nice of you to come and see us! Do come in."

"This is my friend, Julian Boscastle," observed Simon indicating his friend who had a mop of dark hair. "I thought you would not mind if I brought him."

"Not a bit! We're very glad. Would you like something to drink? There's orange, lemon or milk; I'm afraid we don't have coke."

"Orange would be fine, thanks. It's very hot cycling in this weather." They sidled into chairs at the table and regarded the girls through owlish eyes. This is going to be heavy work, thought Bella. What do we do next? But, over the drink and a tin of biscuits, the boys, or at least Simon, became more talkative.

"We really came to see if you would like to go otter hunting. They're meeting over at the Shallows and going down to the river."

"How kind of you! But I don't think I want to come. I would hate to see them catch an otter!"

"Oh they never catch one, do they Bugs?" appealing to his silent friend. "But sometimes people fall in."

"That must be fun!" observed Bella dryly.

"Well it is sometimes. Once it was the master. He must have trod in a hole or something 'cos he went right under. His hat floated off and went down the stream on its own." He moved his hand in circles describing the hat's progress, and both boys spluttered with laughter.

"If you could promise it would happen again I'd come," said Bella. "But I expect it is once in a lifetime, and this time they might catch an otter by mistake, which I shouldn't enjoy at all, so I don't think we'll come."

"Thank you all the same for asking us. Would you like to come back to tea later?" asked Ann. The boys exchanged a sideways glance.

"If you could ask us again another day, we'd like to come," said Simon politely. "But they don't know we're here today, they just think we have gone to the otter hunt. I heard Dad talking so I thought I would like to come and see you. Being in the neighbourhood," he concluded solemnly.

"I see! I could write and invite you to tea, but then your father would wonder where I had met you."

Simon nodded. "If you said you had met me at the otter hunt, that would be different. You can meet anybody there."

"OK then I will write and ask you to tea."

The boys got to their feet. "We'd better go now, because the meet's at eleven. Shall you come just as far as the bridge?"

"I suppose we could do that – just for the sake of verisimilitude!" And the boys grinned at the long word. The girls collected their bicycles.

As the four rode down the lane Simon became more talkative, and the friend more friendly, although still completely silent. When they saw the hounds moving down the stream in the distance, blue-coated followers on either side, the girls turned back.

"Honour is satisfied!" announced Bella firmly. "You can now say that you met us at the hunt and we introduced ourselves. Come and tell us if the Master or Mistress takes a swim."

"I'll write to you," promised Ann. The boys flung their bikes on the ground and sped after the hunt. "Good-oh!" called Simon in flight, but the silent one checked for a moment, turned and called "Thank you for the drink, Miss Cloud."

"So he can speak," mused Ann. "I thought perhaps he'd been chosen as the one who never argues, never quarrels, never contradicts."

"But I bet he packs a hefty punch, probably more effective than words. What did you think of Simon?"

"Nice; but he's a bit afraid of his father, don't you think?"

"Yes. I like him and prefer him to his parent!"

"It feels strange to think that I have cousins," mused Ann. "We have now met Simon. There is Emily who has the bedroom furniture. I wonder if there are others? Perhaps Richard can tell me about them."

"You can ask him tonight but now we must hurry back and get on with our preparations."

Cooking dinner for four may not seem a very difficult task but Ann and Bella had done very little entertaining and were both anxious to have everything just-so. The carpet was set four-square in the middle of the hall and the table and chairs placed exactly symmetrical upon it. Ann had raided the garden and a bunch of late tulips stood proudly in a vase on the table with four sets of cutlery set, straight as guardsmen, on each side.

"We're short of dishes," said Bella. "I think we shall have to serve up in the kitchen."

"Will it be all right if we ask them to come and help themselves?" asked Ann anxiously. They need not have worried. Both Adrian and Richard thoroughly enjoyed the informal meal in the girls' company and talk flowed easily without any embarrassing gaps.

"I made the acquaintance of one of my young cousins this morning," said Ann.

"He had heard his father talking and came to see what we were like," added Bella.

"He said his name was Simon. Is he the youngest? Has he brothers and sisters?"

"Well the eldest is Emily, she got married last year," said Richard.

"I remember! My uncle told me she had the beds and bedding from this house. Are they the only ones?"

"No, Rupert is about seventeen and still at school and Elizabeth, 'Bunty' they call her, is also at school but I don't think they will manage to tame her. She's a real tomboy – crazy about horses! I think you would like her."

"But not the elder ones," surmised Bella.

"Well ..." Richard caught her eye and grinned. "I do not find them very congenial," he admitted.

"That reminds me," said Ann. "My uncle said he had most of the furniture from my house stored in the old stables behind his office. I asked him if the furniture should come to me with the house. He did not seem to know. Said he would have to refer to the will. Do you happen to know what the situation is, Adrian?"

"It cannot be definitely his or he would have taken more care of it," said Bella, shrewdly. "It sounded as if it had all been piled into the outhouses without much protection against damage or damp."

"I will have a talk to my uncle and see what he thinks," promised Adrian.

Bella changed the subject. "Adrian, are you free in August 1st , Bank Holiday Monday?"

"Yes, as far as I know at the moment. Why?"

"Lady Kate and Lord David have asked me to be the 'famous actress' opening their annual summer fete and I thought it would be nice if you came as my 'escort'."

Richard gasped! "You'll never get away with it! You may not have spoken to people in the village much but they have all seen you about!"

"I shall dress for the part of course and be very gracious and slightly condescending; and, if Adrian can wear a velvet smoking jacket and a bow tie and let that nice auburn hair of his grow a little long I think we shall have a great time."

"I haven't said I'll come yet," protested Adrian. "What does it involve? What will I have to do?"

"Nothing really! I shall make a short speech to welcome them, tell them about the good causes they are supporting, drop in a few jokes and wish them a pleasant afternoon."

"Yes – but the 'opener' always walks about and visits every stall and side-show. You could find it expensive," said Richard.

"Lord David has promised me a 'sub' and if I am very charming and chatty perhaps they will not notice if I do not spend very much."

"It sounds quite a lark," said Adrian. "OK. I can't resist. We probably better work out how to fit me into the thespian background." His eyes sparkled as he caught Bella's equally lively glance.

"Oh dear!" said Ann. "I shall be so embarrassed! I don't think I shall go."

"Why not?" asked Richard. "I'll look after you. Just pretend you have never met this fabulous actress before." Bella looked at him. Was he being 'sarky' at her expense? Richard grinned back. He would make sure Ann was not embarrassed.

"I expect I shall be roped in as car park attendant," he said. "You can help me with that."

They took their coffee out onto the terrace and sat chatting in the evening sunshine until Adrian looked at his watch.

"Good heavens! It's past ten already, and I've got to drive back to town. Thank you both for a most enjoyable evening."

Ann and Bella waved goodbye to the smart sports car and the muddy land-rover. "Those two boys are as different as their motors," said Bella. "But they are both nice and I think they enjoyed themselves."

"I like having parties," said Ann. "And I think the house enjoyed it too. Who else can we ask?"

"You could write and ask young Simon and friend to tea on Saturday, and what about Mr Jolly? Do you think he would like to bring his wife to tea on Sunday?"

"Yes, that would be nice, he has been so friendly and helpful."

"We'd better get moving. We have been here six weeks already."

"It does not feel like that. The time has passed so quickly. I suppose our holiday will soon be over," said Ann with a sigh.

Chapter Fifteen

Ann and Bella got busy with plans and preparations for their tea parties. Neither of them had brothers or had had experience of small boys and their appetites.

"I expect they will like sandwiches," said Ann. "Egg, cheese or ham? What do you think?"

"Let's have egg; that will be quite easy with eggs from the farm. I'm sure they both like crisps, and if I make a big fruit cake it will do for both days," said Bella.

"And, do you think scones and a chocolate cake for Sunday?"

"Yes, and we'd better get some coke for the boys."

At 2 o'clock on Saturday Ann went to answer a knock on the front door. She found the two boys standing there with their bicycles abandoned on the drive as before.

"Are we too early?" asked Simon. "We don't need to have tea yet. We wanted lots of time to explore."

"It can't be much different from when your grandmother lived here."

"Oh, we were never able to explore then. She always said she 'could not abide boys fidgeting around'."

"So you never came to see her?"

"Yes; sometimes Dad bought the whole family. Then we had to sit quiet and listen while they talked."

"I see! Well, before you explore why don't you pick your bikes up and park them somewhere. I think the old kitchen would be best." Ann led the way round the corner of the house to the back door through which she and Adrian had broken in on that memorable first visit. It was now normally left open lest frequent opening and shutting should cause it to collapse completely. The boys parked their bikes and stood and looked at the empty barn-like room.

"What a place!" said Simon. "I've never been here before. Do you cook on that big rusty stove?"

"No, there is an electric cooker in the small kitchen in the big house. We use that."

The silent friend was looking up at the roof. "Blue sky!" he said, pointing.

"That's bad," said Simon. "You must get it mended before it rains, otherwise you'll have a flood." He sounded severe. Ann wondered whether she ought to apologize for the state of her property, but explanations would be too complicated, so she led the way back into the yard."Do you want to explore the gardens?" she asked.

"Yes please. Gardens first and then the house."

"Off you go then." Ann walked slowly back into the house to help Bella with washing up and preparations for tea. She wondered what her young cousin, who was obviously used to civilized living with money and servants, would think of her house and garden. Preparations complete she was standing in the hall when Simon came running in calling "Miss Cloud!"

"Yes Simon, what is it?"

"We have been all round your garden and found a big pile of rubbish, branches and things, you ought to tell your gardener to burn them. It is nice and dry and ought to burn well. I can't think why he has not done it."

"Perhaps he has not had time," said Bella, who had joined them in time to hear the implied criticism.

"No, but there's time now," said Ann. "Would you like to help me have a bonfire?"

"Oh, that would be super! You need some matches and some paper to get it going. Come on …" and the boys dashed off followed more slowly by Ann. I need not have worried about keeping them entertained, she thought. In the excitement of tending the blazing fire Simon lost his formality and was happily addressing his new cousin as 'Ann'.

Tea was a picnic. They all sat on the lawn in the sunshine and the boys did full justice to the viands provided. At last Simon spoke, "That was super! Now we would like to explore the house. Please may we Ann?"

"Off you go!" The boys ran up the steps while Ann and Bella remained seated on the grass relaxing and listening to the boys' voices as they explored the rooms of the big house. There was not really all that much to see and they were soon back.

"There is no furniture upstairs at all. Where has it all gone to?"

"I think your sister had it when she got married."

"I remember the wedding last year. That was a good party! Trouble was I had to be all dressed up as a page or something! Bunty was a bridesmaid in a long blue dress with frills. She hated it!" He grinned reminiscently as he remembered the wedding and then returned to his view of the house.

"I don't think much of your drawing room. There's hardly any furniture and no curtains. I can't think why you don't get those dirty walls cleaned and painted, the pictures put back and the curtains hung."

Ann was silent. What could she say? It would take too long to explain. Simon would go back and tell his father. Did it matter? Not really.

Bella had to say something. "What was it like when your Granny lived here?" she asked.

"Oh it was full of furniture. There was a large settee and four big easy chairs and bookcases and a grandfather clock and lots of tables with photographs and ornaments on. I knocked one over once and Grandmother was really shirty."

"Don't you think it is nicer without so much clutter?"

He seemed to consider this. "But where has all the furniture gone?"

"I think it is in the outbuildings behind your father's office."

"Why was it put there?"

"Well it couldn't be left in an empty house, could it?"

He mulled this over, still puzzled. Luckily, the kitten appeared out of the bushes stalking across the lawn towards Ann. "Pussy, pussy, pussy," she called.

"What a lovely kitten!" exclaimed Simon. "Can I stroke it? What is its name?"

"I call him Caesar."

"That's a strange name for a cat!" He lay on the grass beside the little animal and tickled it behind the ears with a gentle finger. "Listen! He's purring, he really likes me!"

Ann was amused at his pleasure. "Have you got a cat at home?"

"No. We've not got any animals. My mother says they make a mess and there's no one to look after them during the week when I am at school."

Time passed quickly. Soon it was six o'clock.

"I think you should go home now," said Ann.

"Yes I suppose so. It's been super! Can we come again next week?"

'"I'm not sure. We may not be here."

"Why? Where are you going? It's your house isn't it?"

"I have to go back to London and get a job."

"A job?" He was still puzzled.

"Never mind, I'll write to you. Come and get your bikes. I'll find you a Mars Bar each to take home."

Sunday afternoon brought a surprise. Just as Ann was welcoming Mr Jolly and being introduced to his wife a dark green Wolsley saloon drove up and stopped beside Mr Jolly's white van. Adrian and Mr and Mrs Nebworth got out of the car.

"I hope it's all right," said Adrian. "But my Aunt was keen to see her furniture in your house and I knew you would not be here much longer."

"Besides, it is such a lovely day," added Mrs Nebworth.

"It's lovely to see you," said Ann. "I should like to show you my garden. Let me introduce Mr and Mrs Jolly. We're having a tea party." The couples were formally introduced and shook hands. Then Ann led the way into the house.

"Take them into the drawing room Ann," said Bella. "I will go and make the tea."

"Would you like some help?" asked Adrian.

When Bella returned carrying the tray she was struck by the feeling that the stage was set with all the actors waiting for the curtain to go up. The two ladies were sitting together on the settee quietly chatting; Mr Nebworth was standing by the window looking out to the garden, and Ann and Mr Jolly were sitting on chairs in the centre of the room.

"This is a very fine room," Mr Jolly was saying, "But a bit dingy. Why don't you have the walls washed down and repainted? I could do it for you if you like."

"That's kind of you," replied Ann. "But I am afraid I can't afford it. I have almost run out of money."

"What have you done with all the money your grandmother left you?"

"She did not leave me any money. I only get the house."

"But she signed a codicil … "

"WHAT!" Mr Nebworth swung round and shouted the word, which echoed round the bare walls of the big room.

"What codicil?" he asked as he picked up a chair and sat down facing Mr Jolly, who was a bit flustered.

"I hope I was not speaking out of turn. We all knows about it in the village."

"Yes, but I don't know," said Mr Nebworth soothingly. "And I am interested. Can you please tell me all about it."

"Well it was over a beer in the Bull one evening. Old Tom Crouch was telling us as how old Mrs Cloud had asked him to go up to the house to sign some papers."

"When was this? Can you remember?"

"It was just after harvest festival, October time, about three weeks before she died."

"Did this man, Tom, tell you anything about the papers?"

"Yes. He said that, when he came into this room with Nellie, his wife, Mrs Cloud was sitting at her desk with a sheet of paper with writing on. "Come in," she said, "I have written a codicil to my will and I want you both to witness my signature." I did not know what a codicil was so I looked it up in my dictionary."

"And what happened to the paper when it was signed?"

"I don't rightly know. Tom did not say."

"Did Tom have any idea of the content?"

"Content?"

"I mean what Mrs Cloud had written?"

"No, of course she did not let him read it, but, as he left he heard her say 'Now the child will have enough money to keep my house safe.' We thought she meant Miss Ann here."

Bella spoke into the silence that followed these words.

"Now then, after that bombshell we'd better have a cup of tea." She put the tray down and started to pour out. Adrian was handing round the cups but Ann was still lost in thought.

"Wake up Ann love and pass the scones round."

Ann came to with a start. "Sorry."

Mrs Nebworth was the first to speak. "It sounds like a fairy tale but I suppose it must be true. Have you met this couple? Are they likely to be reliable witnesses?"

"I haven't met him but she used to come and work for my grandmother. She wanted to work for us but I told her I had no money," said Ann.

"Yes, she is a real character," added Bella. "Said she'd scrub the floors and do the fires and implied that we had let the place get filthy."

"You'd get more sense out of Tom, especially if you get him on his own," claimed Mr Jolly. "He'll be at the Bull come six as usual. You could buy him a beer and talk to him quiet-like."

Mr Nebworth considered this. "Could be a good plan. Best to get it sorted out as soon as possible."

"Shall I come with you?" asked Adrian.

"No, let's not make too much of it. One person is enough." He turned to Mr Jolly. "Can you come and introduce me as if I were just a casual visitor?"

"We shall have to wait and see what happens," said Mrs Nebworth placidly. "What would you do, Ann, if you had some money to spend?"

"I want to buy a bicycle."

"A bicycle?"

"Yes, I have been thinking that, if I got a good job and saved up, I could buy a bicycle and a portable typewriter."

"Going to set up in business are you?" asked Adrian, with a smile.

"Don't tease the girl Adrian. Tell us what you plan to do Ann."

"Well, I suppose it would be a sort of business; I would like to see if I could earn my living going round the country helping farmers with their paperwork. Richard got in an awful muddle with his. Then I could live in the country."

"You could not live on your own in this big house." Bella was a bit scornful.

"No, I should have to find 'digs' somewhere. But, if I kept the house I should be able to work in my garden. Perhaps I could grow vegetables and sell them."

She had obviously been thinking things out, but Bella was rather horrified.

"Oh Ann! I am sure you would not like it. Think how unfriendly people have been!"

"Not every one! There are Richard and Lady Kate and Lord David and Mr and Mrs Jolly here. They are all good friends. I am sure that, when people see me working for my living and not running up bills, they will realize that I am quite different from my grandmother."

"Yes, very different!" said Mr Jolly. "I surely hope it all works out for you."

"The worst bit will be having to go back to work in London. If I do get some money I should not have to do that."

Strange! Thought Adrian. Does she not realize she could get a sizeable sum by selling the house.

Mr Nebworth got to his feet. "It's six o'clock, shall we go and see what Mr Tom Crouch has to say?"

Ann looked at Mrs Nebworth. "Would you like to come and see my garden? It is still very untidy but there are some nice flowers. I can't tell you how grateful I have been for the tools you lent me. Would you like them back?"

"No, I told Adrian to tell you they were spares. You can keep them," said Mrs Nebworth as she followed Ann to the door.

Chapter Sixteen

Things seemed a bit flat on Monday morning. Mr Nebworth had declared himself satisfied that Mrs Cloud had signed a codicil but that was two years ago and Tom Crouch had no idea where the document might be found.

"We shall have to check with her bank," he said."But first of all we must see Mr Cloud."

"Shall I go and see him?" asked Adrian. "I guess his face will be a picture when I tell him." There the matter was left and the visitors departed.

Next morning the girls were finishing their breakfast when a telegram was delivered for Bella.

"This must be about rehearsals," she said as she tore open the envelope. "Yes! Start on Thursday! Oh my goodness! That does not give us much time."

"I suppose we shall have to get all packed up and go."

"Yes, on Wednesday if possible. Let's make a list of everything we have to do." It was quite a lengthy list starting with booking a van to return the furniture, and returning the bicycles to Mr Jolly.

"What will you do about the kitten?" asked Bella.

"I can't take him back to London. Maybe Mary Heriot would have him. Tom Hoby has delivered the milk already this morning, we must be sure and see him on Wednesday."

The furniture van arrived on Wednesday morning to find everything packed and ready. As they started to load up a muddy land-rover swept into the drive and stopped with a jerk. Richard Brent jumped out and strode into the house. Bella was in the hall with two suitcases.

"Where's Ann?" he demanded.

"She's saying goodbye to her garden."

He stormed out through the glass doors and down the terrace to the rose garden. Ann was standing with her back to him in the midst of the scent and colour of the early blossom. He had no time to stop and admire flowers.

"What the hell do you think you're up to?" he demanded. "Tom Hoby says you have cancelled the milk and there's a removal van standing in the drive!"

She turned to face him. Tears were streaming down her face and falling on the bunch of roses she was holding.

"M-my m-money has run out so I've got to get back to L-london and find a j-job," she stammered.

"I think you might have come to tell me and say goodbye."

"I couldn't face it. I was going to write. I could not bear to say goodbye to you."

He put his hands on her shoulders "Why not Ann?"

"Anyway; I did not think that you would mind."

"Mind!" Memories of the last few weeks, ever since he had found Ann with 'flu and kidnapped her flashed through his head. This girl was so different from Julie.

"I don't think I could bear to say goodbye either. Ann – look at me."

"Oh Richard!" she said as he put his arms round her and kissed her gently. He felt thorns from the roses she was holding pricking through his thin shirt and held her away from him to see her face. The tears had stopped as if by magic and she was smiling at him.

"Now what are we going to do?" he asked.

"I shall have to go today," she said.

"And I can't stop we're in the middle of haymaking. Why must you go?"

"Bella starts rehearsals tomorrow and I have to get a job. I used my last shilling paying Tom Hoby for the milk."

"You might have told me last week." He was frowning.

"Saturday?" It seemed a long time ago. "Bella had a telegram on Monday. We've been so busy! Anyway, as I told you, I have no money."

"Yes but … Oh I can't start arguing now! What's the good?" He was cross again. He turned and started to walk away.

"Richard."

He stopped and turned. "Yes?"

"Take care."

That was all. He went back to his haymaking with the words echoing in his mind. It was kind of her to worry about him. He passed Bella without a word, reversed the land-rover and drove off.

Ann came back with her bouquet of roses. She seemed slightly less upset but all she said was, "I must get a good job tomorrow."

That was easier said than done. She started washing dishes after lunch and dinner at a local restaurant but a secretarial post was more difficult to obtain without a reference, which her previous employers were not prepared to provide. So, at nine o'clock on Monday morning she walked into the offices of Merryweather, Nebworth and Merryweather and asked to see Mr Nebworth.

"Have you an appointment?"

"No, but I am a client of his. I am sure he will see me. My name is Anastasia Cloud."

Mr Nebworth viewed his 'client' with interest as she entered the room. He remembered the shy hesitant girl that he had met for the first time nearly three months ago. This young lady walked briskly into the room with a friendly smile. Her cheeks had a fresh colour from outdoor living and she seemed to stand two inches taller.

"Good morning Miss Cloud. It's nice to see you but I am afraid we have no news for you yet."

"News? Oh the codicil. I have not come about that."

"No? I must just tell you that Mr Herbert Cloud has been away all last week. Adrian has an appointment to see him this morning and plans to follow that with a call at the bank. We will be in touch as soon as there is anything definite to tell you."

"Oh, thank you! It doesn't seem real somehow. The reason I came to see you is to ask you if you could give me a reference. I am really a trained shorthand typist and have a certificate to say I can do top speed of 120 words a minute. I have worked as personal secretary to one of the directors of a small company."

He looked at her. "Surely your previous employer could give you a reference."

"Well ... no ... I left in rather a hurry ... he was ..." her embarrassed flush was more explicit than the words. "I slapped his face," she added.

"Good for you! I understand the problem."

Just then there was a knock on the door and a woman came in and put a pile of papers on his desk.

"Good morning Mr Nebworth. Here is your post. It is a pity there is such a lot with Jane away."

"Thank you Doreen, I will deal with it later." She left the room and Mr Nebworth turned to Ann. "That makes two problems. One; how can I give you a reference when I have not seen your work, and two; how can I get this pile of correspondence cleared with my secretary on holiday this week?"

Ann caught his drift. "Would you like me to take down and type your letters for you?" she asked. "I would be pleased to help."

"We'll make a deal. If you do a good job this morning, and I am sure you will, you can work here for the rest of the week. On Friday you will get pay and a reference. Will that do?"

"Oh thank you, I am so very much obliged to you."

An astute businessman, Mr Nebworth was looking to the future. If Miss Cloud did inherit from her grandmother she would probably be glad of help and advice, which would, of course, be provided by Messrs Merryweather, Nebworth and Merryweather

As she travelled home in the tube that evening Ann reviewed her day. Some of the legal terms were new to her but Mr Nebworth seemed quite pleased with her work. Mrs Dale had tea ready when she got in and was interested to hear about her activities.

After tea Ann disappeared upstairs to her attic room. She had a letter to write. It was important to set the right tone without the distraction of her aunt's chatter. The room was small but the bed was comfortable, there were shelves along one wall for her possessions and a small easy chair. The evening sun shining in through the small window lighted up the room but it was all so different from Cloud's End. Ann gave a small sigh as she sat down on the easy chair with a notepad on her knee.

Dear Richard,

Here I am back in London in my small bedroom wishing that I were at Cloud's End with my garden and my friends.

I am sorry I did not tell you we had to leave but I was so busy and thinking of saying goodbye made it all seem so final somehow.

I am determined to get a good job so that I can save enough to buy a bicycle and a portable typewriter. Do you think I could make a living going round the farms and stables as a part-time secretary? That is what I mean to try.

This morning I went to see Mr Nebworth, Adrian's uncle. His secretary is on holiday this week so I am filling the gap. On Friday he will give me my pay and a reference. Then I can go looking for a permanent post. I make some extra by washing dishes at a local restaurant every evening but I think it will be a long time before I get back to Cloud's End.

Unless – let me tell you. Such a strange thing happened that last Sunday at Cloud's End. We had invited Mr and Mrs Jolly to tea. They have been so helpful, and then Adrian arrived with his uncle and aunt, Mr and Mrs Nebworth because Mrs Nebworth wanted to see the furniture she had lent us.

While we were talking Mr Jolly happened to say that my grandmother had signed a codicil, which the village all thought that meant she had left me some money.

Just think! It would mean I could come back to live there! Mr

Nebworth was on to it like a shot and has told Adrian to go and see my uncle, but nothing can be done without the document itself, surely it should have turned up by now, so I am not banking on it. Time to go and do my washing up. I will post this on my way. Don't work too hard dear Richard.

Take care
Ann.

Mrs Bunce was worried about Richard. Lady Kate heard about it from Harriet. "I was at the WI last night and Ivy Bunce was telling me how hard Mr Richard was working. He hardly stops all day and keeps going all hours."

"Perhaps he is making the most of the fine weather. It is ideal for haymaking at present."

"Yes, but it is more than that. It's like when his engagement was broken off, he can't seem to relax."

"Has he got another girl?"

"Well, Ivy said she had great hopes of Miss Ann Cloud. They argued at times but she seemed to understand him and now she's gone off back to London and left him in a right tizzy."

"I did not realize the girls had gone. Is Cloud's End shut up again?"

"Yes. Bill Jolly told Ivy the furniture van came and took every last thing away."

"I see. It seems as if Richard needs my help. We will ask him over for a meal one evening next week."

Chapter Seventeen

Nellie Crouch was upset, Tom was upset; they were both upset, but, unlike him, she intended to do something about it. She dressed herself in her best skirt, a heavy black broadcloth she had bought at a jumble sale on the sworn testimony that it had belonged to Mrs Heriot's mother, and so was suitable wear for best. Over this she chose a rubbed velvet jacket with a narrow edge of fur to the collar, a brightly coloured scarf, and, with a long hatpin, skewered a black straw hat to the top of her head. She thrust her feet into the heavy boots she always wore to walk along the lanes and picked up her bulky handbag, which she slung over one shoulder.

She stumped down the stairs and out of the door. Tom was at the bottom of the garden disconsolately prodding the ground with a fork. This was his usual defence against the world's trials.

She screeched at him, "Yer dinner's in the oven. I'll be back later."

He regarded her sombrely. Up to mischief she was; he recognized the signs. "Do us all a harm you will," he muttered. "Better leave it alone. Least said soonest mended."

Nellie ignored him and strode off across the common carrying on a one-sided conversation. "Old bastard! I'll show yer! Think you can ride rough-shod over all! I'll show yer! Nobody can't frit me with bad words, nor make me the scapegoat for their own evil!" She was still muttering when she reached Mallow Hampton castle, crossed the yard, and poked her head in at the kitchen door. She had an old enemy in the cook and eyed her sternly.

"His lordship a'tome?" she demanded. "I want for to see him."

"Do you indeed! And perhaps you'll kindly tell me what you want him for Nellie Crouch. He ain't got time to waste on the likes of you."

"I aint got time to bandy words with you, Sarah Falls. 'Tis the noble lord I got to see not any handmaidens!" At this masterpiece of language Sarah was momentarily struck dumb, and Lady Kate, an enthralled listener, quietly intervened.

"Good morning Ellen. Did you want to see my son? He is in the garden at the moment. Come with me I'll take you to him."

"Thank you my lady." Nellie was suitably humble as she followed Lady Kate out into the garden.

"Ellen wants to see you on business, David. I think you had better take her into the study, "said Lady Kate and smiled at his raised eyebrows and look of surprise.

"Of course, please bring her with you." This was definitely a hint that he wished her to be present at the interview. As she said later, she would not have missed it on any account! To her, Nellie was always good value, and this time she surpassed herself in hints, allusions, Biblical quotations and downright bad language.

At last Lord David interrupted her. "Do I understand that Mr Cloud came to see you this morning and actually threatened you with imprisonment? But for what reason Mrs Crouch? This is a serious matter and we must be sure of our facts."

"For this, your lordship! 'Tis a lie, all a lie, he ses! You aint never wrote your names on nawthen, he ses, he'll put us in gaol if us says we had. So I d'aint argue with the sour old devil. I'll take it straight to the noble lord, I ses to myself, and he shall do what he think right." She put her bulky shoulder bag on the table and started sorting through it, taking out the contents as she did so. Lady Kate and her son watched amazed as the squirrel's hoard was spread out in front of them. A pair of worn leather gloves, a shabby purse that spilled coppers from a tear down one side, a grubby man's handkerchief, a comb with several teeth missing, a packet of peanuts and, at last "Found it!" exclaimed the hoarder and waved a grubby envelope before their eyes.

Lord David took a sheet of paper from the envelope and, with a startled gasp, read out. "Codicil to the will of Emily Jane Cloud!"

"That's right," said Nellie Crouch. "Codicil she called it. She signed first then me and Tom had to sign after, 'as witnesses' she said."

"Then she gave it to you to keep?" asked Lady Kate.

"That's right. She said not to tell no-one nothing about it."

"Quite right," said Lord David. "And now you have brought it to me and I will look after it."

"You won't tell that 'Erbert I give it to you. I don't want for him to put me in prison."

"There is no danger of that," said Lady Kate. "And now you must have something to eat before your long walk back. Come into the kitchen and Sarah will give you some tea and a sandwich."

When Lady Kate came back into the study she found her son standing lost in thought the document still in his hand. "This could be tricky!" he said. "It is a legacy of ten thousand pounds to her granddaughter Anastasia Cloud."

"Why, the girl will be thrilled!"

"Of course. But I know someone who will not be at all pleased."

"Herbert Cloud!"

"Exactly!"

"Do you think he will contest it?"

"That is a possibility."

"Do you remember that young man who turned up at Cloud's End in that extraordinary croquet costume? I think Ann said he was in his uncle's law firm."

"That could be a useful contact. Do you remember the name?"

"No, but we can always ask Ann."

"Better not raise her hopes before we are sure it will hold water."

"We can't do anything more about it at present, and don't forget, we have Richard Brent coming to dinner this evening."

"Yes, I remember! We have got to cheer him up."

But Richard did not seem to need any cheering up. "I've had a letter from Ann," he said. "She wants to buy a bicycle and there is a most extraordinary story about a codicil to old Mrs Cloud's will."

"That's right!" said Lord David. "I have it here."

"How on earth? Ann said the document was missing."

"Nellie Crouch turned up with it this afternoon and gave it to David."

"Apparently Herbert Cloud went to see them threatening all sorts of penalties so she decided it was safer to bring it to me."

"What are you going to do?

"I should be happier presenting it to Herbert Cloud with some sort of legal back-up."

"Why don't you contact Adrian? He is the lawyer who found Ann and told her about the house."

"I would if I knew his address."

"Ann mentions the uncle in her letter. I am sure she gave his name. Hang on, let me look." He took an envelope out of his breast pocket and skimmed through the contents. "Yes, it is Mr Nebworth."

"Nebworth! A London firm of course. I am sure I can get in touch with him."

Chapter Eighteen

Once again that staid young lawyer, Mr Adrian Peel, was walking along the dingy London street towards No. 25. The pinstripe suit, the brief case and the bowler hat were the same but there was a spring in his step and a sparkle in his eye that belonged to a bearer of good news.

Mrs Dale answered his knock. "Why! It's Mr Peel! I expect you've come to see Ann, she's just got back. Come along in love." She led the way into the room where the table was laid for tea as before. Ann was sitting by the fire. He thought she looked a bit dejected but she stood up and welcomed him with a smile.

"Hello Adrian. It's nice to see you. Will you join us for tea?"

"Yes, I would be pleased to, but first I must tell you the good news."

"Good news?" queried Auntie Lou. "That would cheer us up. Here's Ann been out all day looking for a job."

"No luck?" he asked sympathetically.

"No luck," she confirmed.

"Never mind; perhaps you can make do with a legacy."

"Legacy?" exclaimed Auntie Lou, while Ann said more quietly, "So the codicil has been found?"

"Yes. Nellie Crouch had it hidden somewhere and took it to Lord David at Mallow Hampton Castle. Your grandmother left you ten thousand pounds and the furniture from the house."

Ann gasped "I can't believe it! What did my uncle say?"

"He was not pleased. In fact there is some difficulty. The residue of Mrs Cloud's estate, after Death Duties, was used to fund trusts for each of his four children, so the money is not readily available. I have here a cheque for one thousand pounds. The balance will follow."

"One thousand pounds!" Ann was still reeling, "That's more than four years salary!"

As she sat trying to relate to such a large sum, whatever would she find to spend it on? Adrian thought over the day's events. Lord David had met him that morning in the lounge of the White Hart in Mallow Greatham with the codicil. Adrian had studied the document carefully. "It seems watertight to me," he had said.

Lord David voiced his concern. "I rather think Herbert Cloud will try to contest it."

"The only grounds he could have would be if she was not of sound mind. It must have been only a few weeks before she died. There is no possibility of Ann having influenced her, she barely knew that the girl existed."

Adrian had made a brief phone call to ensure that Herbert Cloud was free, then they walked down the high street to his office.

Mr Cloud received them with a hostile stare. "A deputation I see!" he said. "To what do I owe this honour My Lord and …"

Lord David broke in "This is Mr Adrian Peel. He represents Miss Ann Cloud."

"Yes," added Adrian. "I have come to tell you that the codicil has been found. Mrs Cloud left her granddaughter ten thousand pounds and the furniture of the house."

Mr Cloud snatched the paper out of Adrian's hand and stood reading it.

"Do you think we might sit down?" asked Lord David.

"Of course, of course, take a seat. This is going to require some very careful consideration. In the first place, where did you find it? It seems very strange that it should turn up after all these months."

"It was brought to me by Nellie Crouch last Friday."

"Nellie Crouch! You can't believe a word that woman says. When I saw her on Friday morning she swore blind she had never ever heard of it."

"Perhaps she preferred to bring it to me."

"You're not expecting to rely on the evidence of that scatty woman in a court of law?"

"I don't think it will come to that."

"Perhaps you can tell us, Mr Cloud," broke in Adrian, "whether you recognize the signature. I am sure that you must have examples here that we can compare with the signature on the document."

"I have to admit that it does look like her writing but, look here, it was only three weeks before she died. She can't have been in her right mind."

"I expect the doctor will be able to confirm her mental state. Maybe we can contact him." Mr Cloud looked at Lord David. They both knew that old Mrs Cloud had been mentally alert until the day she died. He then sat looking down at the document. At last he spoke in more reasoned tones.

"You have to understand this presents me with a problem. Death Duty Tax took a large part of my mother's estate. I discussed this with my wife and we decided to set up trust funds for my four children to reduce future liabilities.

"I am sure that was a very prudent thing to do," said Adrian. "But it does not remove the onus on the executors of Mrs Cloud's estate to pay this legacy to Miss Ann Cloud in accordance with her grandmother's wishes."

Mr Cloud seemed to accept the situation. "Yes but I cannot raise such a large sum immediately. I shall have to talk to my wife and decide the best way of meeting the liability. The best I can do at present is to give you a cheque for one thousand pounds for my niece."

"I am sure my client will accept that," said Adrian. "But, obviously, she will want to know when she will get the balance. Perhaps you will keep me informed on your progress."

Mr Cloud glared at him. Bumptious young upstart! The implication was clear, no good trying to negotiate easier terms with the niece.

Adrian did not feel it necessary to give Ann more details of this interview but now produced a letter from Lady Kate. "Lord David gave me this to give you. I expect it is to congratulate you."

As Ann slit open the envelope the door opened and Bella came in.

"Hello folks!" she said cheerfully, and continued "Why! Here's Adrian! That's nice! Did you come to see me?"

Adrian grinned at her. "No, I came to see Ann."

"That's a put-down! I think I shall take offence."

"Adrian came to tell Ann that her grandmother left her ten thousand pounds," said Mrs Dale.

Ann looked up from the letter she was reading. "Lady Kate writes to congratulate me and has invited me to stay over the bank holiday weekend."

"That will be nice," said her aunt. "But you will have to smarten yourself up a bit."

"Oh dear! Do you think I ought not to go?"

"Of course you must go," said Bella bracingly. "You saw what it was like when we went to tea. No butler or footmen – just that nice Harriet."

"I suppose I can spend some of this money on some nice new clothes. Oh, and, Bella, Lady Kate has invited you and Adrian to lunch on August Bank Holiday."

"Good! Then we can make our way through the lanes and creep in the back way."

"Are you getting cold feet?" asked Adrian.

"No, but that motor of yours is very distinctive and has been seen in the village often enough to be recognized."

"Which you won't be?"

"Well, if I dress up with plenty of make-up and wear a hat it will take a bit longer."

"Crazy kid!" but it was obvious that Adrian was looking forward to the adventure just as much as Bella.

Ann had a more important problem. She sat holding the cheque between the tips of her fingers. "What should I do with this?" she asked. "Do I have to spend it all on the house?"

"No. There were no conditions laid down with the bequest, so you can spend it any way you like. I presume you want to keep the house and make it habitable?"

"Oh yes. The house and the garden go together. That garden is far the best thing I ever had in my life."

"Do you mean you really want to go and live out in the wilds?" Mrs Dale was incredulous, but Bella knew Ann better.

"You fell for the garden the moment you saw it. Didn't you?" she said.

"Yes. I never had a garden before."

"Where do you keep your money at present?" asked Adrian.

"In the Post Office, when I have any."

"Put this in the Post Office then. You can withdraw such sums as you require; when the balance becomes available we can think about investing part of it."

"Won't it all be needed to repair the house?"

"I shouldn't think so. You'll need an investment income to live on."

"I shall have to get a job. With a bicycle and typewriter I can go round helping farmers with their forms and paperwork."

"Well, don't rush in before you have had a chance to look around. There is no hurry with that money behind you." Bella's wise advice was acknowledged by Adrian with a grin. "Look who's talking!" he said, but continued, "She is right Ann. Give it a bit of time and enjoy your house and garden."

That night Ann lay awake in her attic room for some time. She found her good fortune awesome and was a little scared when she tried to look into the future. What would Richard think of it? She wondered as she drifted off to sleep.

Chapter Nineteen

Lord David was walking down Mallow Greatham high street. Having left Herbert Cloud's office and said goodbye to Adrian, he now had some commissions to carry out for his mother. A woman cycling towards him stopped and dismounted. It was Janet Crane.

"Hello David," she said. "Did Lady Kate get my letter? Will you be able to come and help celebrate my father's birthday?" Lord David was puzzled. This Janet seemed different.

"Is it *de rigueur* to cycle in jodhpurs these days?" he asked.

"I'm wearing jodhpurs because I have been working all morning at Jerry Jackson's stables. I've got a job. But you didn't answer my question."

"I'm sorry. What was it you wanted to know?"

"I am planning a small dinner party to celebrate my father's sixty fifth birthday. He is not retiring but hopes to take life easier now he has a young assistant. I wrote to Lady Kate and hope you will both be able to join us next Friday."

"I expect my mother will be writing to you. As far as I know we are both free. Thank you." He raised his cap and walked on. Janet would have been pleased to know that, instead of taking her for granted as he always had in the past, he was now trying to decide how it was that she seemed different.

Janet cycled through Mallow Greening village and propped her bike against the vicarage wall. She entered the house and called out "Mary."

"Coming," replied Mary Heriot as she ran down the stairs. "Have you come to lunch? Ernest is out so I am on my own."

"Well, I really came to ask you both to dinner next Friday. It is my father's sixty fifth birthday and I think we should celebrate."

"Of course! It is an important landmark. Who else is coming?"

"Jerry Jackson and his wife have accepted. I wrote to Lady Kate and asked her and David. I saw him in town this morning and asked if they could come. He seemed rather vague, so I don't know. I shall be so disappointed if he can't come."

"And you have bought a new outfit specially for the occasion! Tell me what it is like."

"Now that I am working I have some money to spend. I went to Harrods!"

"Did you? That was brave!"

"I got a long silky pleated navy skirt, it whispers as I walk, and a cream silk blouse to wear with my mother's gold chain. I hope that will be all right. I did not want anything too flowery."

"That sounds ideal. I shall be interested to see it."

"You will be able to come?"

"Yes, of course. We do not get many social occasions these days."

"I have also asked Andy Fletcher, my father's new assistant. It will be helpful for him to get to know people."

Janet Crane's plans for her dinner party all came to fruition. Lady Kate and Lord David accepted. Mr Crane claimed she was making a lot of fuss about nothing, but, as she realized, was really very pleased to have a celebration and see his friends. There was much consultation between Janet and Mary about the most suitable menu and all was set for a pleasant evening.

As they sat at the dining table there was plenty of news to share. Lady Kate entertained them with a description of Nellie Crouch's visitation and Lord David followed with Mr Herbert's reaction to the news that he had to pay ten thousand pounds to Mrs Cloud's other granddaughter.

"I wonder what Ann will do now she has all that money? " said Mary. "I am looking after her kitten for her."

"Is she planning to sell the house?" asked Janet.

"We shall find out next week," said Lady Kate. "I have asked her to stay over Bank Holiday week-end."

"Of course, we have the Fete on Bank Holiday Monday," said the vicar. "How are the arrangements going?"

"Pretty well I think," said David. "The Mallow Greatham Brass Band is booked and also two coaches to bring the band and anyone else who wants to come. All we need is a fine day."

"I see you have a famous actress to open it," said Edna Jackson. "I hope she is not charging too high an appearance fee."

"No. I am sure she will be very suitable." Lord David decided to change the subject. The fewer people knew the actual identity of the "opener" beforehand the better.

"I saw Phill with his arm in plaster last week," he said. "Does any one know if he had an accident?"

"Why, yes," replied Jerry with a chuckle. "It was quite bizarre! You know he has bought this new horse and trap in order to enter in driving competitions?"

"I heard they had a course set up in a field the other side Mallow Greatham a couple of weeks ago."

"That's right. Phill was just coming away down the lane when he saw another competitor driving Shetland ponies coming towards him. For some ungodly reason that horse of his really hates Shetland ponies! Phill pulled into the side of the lane to give them plenty of room to pass."

"I would have pushed on to get past as soon as possible," commented David.

"Perhaps that would have been better, but Phill is not very experienced. Anyway; while they were standing there, a horse leaned over the fence and bit Phill's horse. All hell broke loose! The horse bucked and then took off down the lane at a gallop. Phill was thrown out and broke his arm, Luckily, the groom had already dismounted."

"I hope it did not cause a serious accident," said Lady Kate.

"No; the horse jumped over the gate at the T junction and there it was, held, with the trap still in the lane."

"I expect the trap was badly damaged."

"No, it was not damaged at all. Phill picked himself up and, somehow got over the fence, calmed his horse and undid the harness. Only then did he realize that his arm was damaged."

"Was the horse hurt," asked Janet.

Her father answered her. "No, surprisingly enough there was no damage. Phill called me in to check over for strains and sprains and I found nothing."

"It will hate Shetland ponies even more from now on," said David with wry smile.

"Yes, it will think the ponies were responsible for the bite. That's the way a horse's mind works," said Jeff.

"Horses can be queer," said Andy. "My father was in the TA before the war, artillery. At the annual training camp at Blackpool he was riding down the road to the beach in front of a gun-carriage drawn by four horses when they came across some donkeys. His horse bucked and swung round, right into the gun carriage team, causing utter chaos. My father found out afterwards that that horse hated donkeys. No one had told him; although he probably would not have been able to stop the horse. Anyway, he ended up in hospital with a crushed knee."

"I hope the damage was not permanent," said Lady Kate.

"I don't think so. He seems to move about a tennis court pretty smartish. When I am home we have some good matches."

"Probably catch up with him as he gets older," said Mr Crane. "That's the trouble with old injuries."

When people whose life is lived with horses get together they talk horse. Janet's dinner party was no exception to this rule. Even Janet relaxed and kept her friends amused with some stories of her adventures working as groom at Jerry's stables. Of course Jerry pretended to be surprised at these activities.

David decided that the evening was proving more entertaining than he had anticipated. As he got up to go he remembered the fete and asked Jerry if he could bring two or three horses to the castle. "They need to be quiet," he said. "We are charging a shilling a time for rides round the field, and," turning to Janet, "will you be able to come and help look after them as usual?"

"Yes I've got that booked and have asked Bunty Cloud to come and help as well."

"Do you think she will?" asked Lady Kate. "Her mother will expect her to come dressed in her best 'garden party' clothes."

"Mrs Cloud will not be able to stop her bringing riding clothes and changing at the castle," predicted Lord David.

Chapter Twenty

On Bank Holiday Friday Ann was met at Mallow Greatham station by Lord David. Once in the castle she was welcomed by Lady Kate, who

drawing room when you are ready, we have
aid as she went out and left Ann to examine her
seemed five times the size of the little attic
London and, although the room she and Bella
ıd was large, their camping out arrangements
nd luxury of this room. There was a big double
window, an easy chair by the fireplace and a
and dresser.
tried sitting in the armchair and then went to
This is living!" she said to herself. Then she
opened her suitcase. On top was a cream
shaped neckline and puffed sleeves. She had
ear for dinner in the evenings and hoped it
Next she unpacked a new cotton dress and
ern on a lavender background, and was, she
the fete, as representative of her house,

Eventually, wearing her new silk dress, with shining hair and smart make-up, she went down to the drawing room. "Could I ever make Cloud's End like this?" she said to herself as she went and sat down where she could look out of the window. She was quite glad to be on her own for a while to get accustomed to the new milieu where, she supposed, her life would lie in the future.

Lady Kate had invited Richard to dinner. She thought he would be pleased to see Ann but had not told him Ann would be there. He was a bit harassed, milking had seemed to take for ever that evening and he had had a rush to get ready. He was not feeling very sociable.

Lady Kate met him in the hall. "Go on into the drawing room," she said. "We will be along shortly." She then went to join Lord David in the study.

"Give them ten minutes," she said.

Ann looked up as the door opened.

"Richard!" she exclaimed, as she stood up.

He was equally surprised. "Ann!" he said. They stood in silence for a short time. Then …

"Wherever did you come from?"

"I never expected to see you!"

They both spoke at once. Their laughter broke the tension.

"Oh! Ann, my darling! I've missed you so much!" Somehow she was in his arms and he was kissing her.

When Lady Kate came to tell them dinner was served she was pleased to see they were sitting together on the settee. Richard's arm was round Ann's shoulders.

"You look very comfortable!" she commented.

"We are comfortable," said Richard.

"He asked me to marry him," said Ann shyly. "And I said yes. Do you think that will be all right?"

"Of course, my dear. I was expecting it," said Lady Kate. "Now come along and have your dinner."

Once dinner was served lady Kate expressed her interest in Ann's future plans.

"When will the wedding be?" she asked.

"Oh, I haven't thought about that, and," with a shy smile at Richard, "we did not discuss any date."

"You won't have to go back to London, will you?"

"No, I thought I might ask Mary Heriot if I could rent a room at the vicarage. She has got my kitten already."

"Good, then you will be handy to supervise work on the house."

"I expect that will take time. I want to buy a bicycle then I can go round the farms with my portable typewriter and deal with their forms and correspondence."

"I suppose that might be a way of getting to know people."

"Yes. I have had some leaflets printed and thought I could hand them out to everyone who comes to the fete."

There was a moment of awestruck silence. Lady Kate had a vision of old Mrs Cloud's horror if she found her granddaughter touting for business like a commercial traveller at a fun fair.

Richard could never be tactful.

"My dear girl! You can't possibly do that. Everyone will think you are just a cheap typist looking for business."

"Well, I am looking for business. Why not?"

"My dear, don't forget you are the owner of Cloud's End, Mrs Cloud's granddaughter. You don't want to start by making a bad impression."

"You don't think it a good idea? But I shall need to earn some money."

"What about the legacy?"

"I don't know how much I shall need to spend on the house." She was a bit dashed by their reaction, and changed tack."Do you think it will be OK for me to buy a bicycle?"

"I'll take you in to Mallow Greatham tomorrow," offered Richard.

"Yes, you do that, Richard, and make sure it is a good one," said Lady Kate.

Next morning we find Richard and Ann standing in the middle of the drawing room at Cloud's End. Ann was visualizing it with clean, painted walls, long velvet curtains and similar furniture to that at the castle.

"I wonder if I shall ever live here," she said.

"You are going to live at Shallowford with me," said Richard.

"I know but it's a bit dark and dismal, isn't it?" she said without thinking.

His ready temper flared up.

"So that's what you think is it! Now that you have been invited to stay at the castle and have money to live it up, my home is not good enough! You're turning into a typical 'stuck up Cloud'!" He was struck by her silence and turned to look at her. Her face had gone white.

"I'm sorry," she faltered. "I didn't mean to criticize. Please don't take it like that." There were tears in her eyes and a doleful droop to her mouth. "Had I better sell the house and forget all about it?"

Her evident distress was the best way of defusing the situation.

There was only one thing for him to do. He pulled her into his arms and kissed her.

"I'm sorry too! Forget I said it. It's early days yet. We have to find out how to live together."

Ann's nature was less volatile than Richard's. She found it difficult to put the spat out of her mind.

"Yes, I suppose so," she said doubtfully.

There was one way of changing the subject. "Come out and see the garden," he said. "The roses are still covered in flowers."

"Are they? Let's go out and see." She led the way out through the glass doors.

"Richard!" she exclaimed. "The grass has been cut. It looks like a real croquet lawn. Did you do it?"

Yes. I had a bit of spare time and brought my scythe up here. I thought it would improve the look of the place," he said in an offhand manner.

"Oh, thank you. It makes such a difference." She was puzzled. Had he done it for her? He was such a strange young man. Later that morning she had another surprise.

After the bicycle had been purchased Richard drove her back to Shallowford farm for lunch. Mrs Bunch welcomed them at the kitchen door.

"Come along in my dearies. Lunch is just ready. I expect you are both hungry."

Ann was not listening. She stood and looked at the room. The old walls had been freshly whitewashed, all plants and clutter had been moved from the windowsills; the curtains had been washed and hung crisp and clean either side; the copper pans and horse brasses that hung from the beams were polished and sparkling and the table was laid with a clean white cloth and blue willow pattern china. In addition there was the appetizing aroma of the stew bubbling away on the stove. It was all bright and fresh and clean. In her surprise she stood speechless wondering what she could say that would not cause offence.

Mrs Bunch addressed her. "I can see you're right amazed my dear. I'll tell you what happened. Come July life seemed a bit flat and dull with nothing to do in the nice light evenings, so me and Mr Richard put our heads together and got going to brighten up the place a bit."

Ann found courage to comment. "It's lovely," she said, smiling up at Richard.

"That's right. Now come and sit down and – oh my goodness, I'll forget my head next! – I've never congratulated you Miss Ann. Mr Richard told me last night you had promised to marry him. I was so pleased. I hope you will both be very happy. I have always felt you were just the right girl for Mr Richard."

On Sunday morning Ann accompanied Lady Kate and Lord David to church. Lady Kate was wearing a hat, so Ann was pleased she had a hat with her. The silk pansies decorating the navy straw were an exact match with the lavender of her dress and jacket. She felt that being suitably dressed for the occasion would give her courage if she were introduced to a number of new people.

Once in church she looked round for Richard but could not see him. Does he ever go to church? she wondered. Then, just as they were standing up for the first hymn, there were quick steps down the aisle. It was Richard. He edged into the pew to stand next to her.

Throughout the service Ann was conscious of the masculine presence beside her. What will it be like to be married she wondered. It would change her whole life.

As they stood up to go after the service, Richard said hurriedly. "I can't stop. One of my cows is going to calve any moment." He bent and kissed her and was gone, sliding quickly between the chattering groups.

Lady Kate looked at Ann's flushed face and said. "Oh dear! Now we shall have everyone putting two and two together and having a good gossip. You and Richard will have to be sure to make a formal announcement at the fete tomorrow."

Then Mary Heriot came up to speak to them. "Good! I hoped you would be here Ann. I wonder if you would come and help with the teas at the fete tomorrow. We are short staffed and are desperate to get more help."

"I shall be pleased to help if you think I would be of use. I've never served in a café but I've done plenty of washing up." Ann was pleased to think she would be well away from the embarrassment of watching Bella open the fete, and also out of Richard's company until they were ready to make that important announcement.

Chapter Twenty-one

On August 1st Ann woke to the sound of activity outside her open window. She got out of bed and looked out. A gang of men was busy erecting a marquee on the large flat lawn at the side of the house. Was it a tennis lawn? She wondered. It was much bigger than the croquet lawn at Cloud's End. She dressed and went downstairs. When she entered the dining room she was greeted by Harriet.

"Good morning Miss Ann. Can I get you a boiled egg with your toast and coffee? Her Ladyship and Mr David had their breakfast early and are now busy outside."

"Oh!" Ann was not used to being waited on but Harriet had such a kind smile she could not be shy. "A boiled egg would be very nice if it is not too much trouble," she said.

"No trouble at all. Do you like it soft or hard boiled?"

"Not too hard please."

After breakfast Ann went outside to explore. She was amazed at the bustle of activity. Tables were being set up; strings of flags streamed between tall poles; stacks of chairs were disappearing into the marquee. She found Lord David knocking in stakes.

"What are these for?" she asked. "Is there anything I can do to help?"

"Hello," he greeted her. "This is the track for the children's races. Do you see that rope there? Could you tie it along the tops of these posts?"

"What a lot of work for just one afternoon," she commented.

"Perhaps it is, but, if we put on a good show and folks enjoy themselves we shall raise enough money to keep the village going and get a good crowd next year. Anyway it only takes one day even if it is a bit hectic."

Ann considered this. She had tended to think Lord David as very pleasant but rather laid back and casual. Quite different from Richard in fact; but possibly just as effective in getting things done. She knew Richard had to be busy at work that morning and would be organizing the car park while she had agreed to help in the tea tent that afternoon.

The previous evening Lady Kate had taken Richard to task. "You can't go kissing the girl in public like that without setting the whole village gossiping! If you are both serious I think you should announce your engagement at the fete tomorrow, and," turning to Ann, "I am assuming you are over 21, but haven't you any relations that would like to be introduced to Richard first?"

"Well, there's my Uncle Herbert," said Ann doubtfully. "But I don't think he would be really interested."

"What about Bella?" asked Lord David. "She is your cousin."

"Of course. She and her mother my Auntie Lu, are my only family. They will both be here tomorrow. I know Auntie Lu will be thrilled to hear of my romance; though very doubtful about my burying myself in the country. She's like Bella, very forthright. I'm sure you'll like her Richard."

"I suppose the most important thing is – will she like me?" said Richard.

"Of course she will. Just don't make any personal remarks about her hair. It varies from gold to auburn depending on how she feels when she visits the hairdresser."

Fortunately Mrs Dale had not been too adventurous with hair colour. The curls piled on the top of her head were a reasonably discreet honey colour, but there was no doubt in Lord David's mind when he saw her and Mr Darcy alight from the bus with the band and other visitors from Mallow Greatham.

"Are you Mrs Dale, Ann's Aunt?" he asked. "Come along and find Ann, she has some news for you." He took them into the tea tent and went off to the car park, where he found Richard talking to two strangers who had just emerged from a dark green Wolsley and went up to introduce himself.

"Good afternoon. I'm David Mallow Hampton. Have you come to our fete? You'll find it a very hum-drum village affair I'm afraid."

"My nephew Adrian is here as escort to Isobel Duncan," said the gentleman.

"And it is such a fine day for a run out into the country, now we are no longer restricted by petrol rationing," added his wife.

Recognition dawned. "You must be Mr Nebworth," said Lord David. "I spoke to you about the codicil to Mrs Cloud's will."

"Yes, we thought we would come on an unofficial visit so to speak."

"That's fine. Now Richard, why don't you take Mr and Mrs Nebworth to the tea tent to find Ann. She is waiting for you. I will take care of the car park for a short time."

Mrs Dale had received Ann's news with congratulations and a warm hug.

"Here comes Richard," said Ann. "I do hope you'll like him."

"Well young man! What excuse do you have for planning to bury my niece in the country?"

"But I like it Auntie!" put in Ann.

"Let him speak for himself."

"I love Ann and it makes me happy to think she loves me and wants to share my life."

"Well now, when young Mr Peel first came to tell Ann about the house I wondered what the future had in store for her, but I never thought of a country wedding."

Then Mrs Nebworth came forward with an outstretched hand for Richard and a kiss for Ann.

"Congratulations both of you. I do hope we shall be invited to the wedding."

Then an announcement came over the loud-speaker.

"Welcome to Mallow Hampton Castle. Would you all please gather on the lawn in front of the house to meet Miss Isabel Duncan, who will perform the opening ceremony""

"Our Bella!" exclaimed Mrs Dale. "I must go and see this. Come on Fred."

Ann hung back while all the other helpers crowded round the entrance of the tent to watch. As Mary Hislop watched Bella step out through the long window onto the wooden dais she wondered how soon it would be before this elegant lady with her big flowery hat, slinky flared skirt and high heeled shoes would be connected with the casually dressed cousin who had accompanied Ann into the village.

The young man who followed Bella out fitted the part of "escort" perfectly, with his smart navy reefer jacket and maroon bow tie. His auburn hair shone with brylcream and – was there just a hint of make-up to emphasize eyebrows, lips and tan? Mrs Nebworth was amazed at this 'larger than life' nephew. By her side her husband was grunting.

"Look at the boy! Taking up with an actress! He'll want to go on the stage next!"

"I know he enjoys his amateur dramatics, but I am sure he will want to keep his job."

"I certainly hope you are right!"

Bella spoke clearly and to the point. Her efforts were rewarded with a polite round of applause as people moved away to patronize the stalls and side-shows and enjoy walking round the park in the summer sunshine.

Ann enjoyed her stint serving teas. Mary Hislop had introduced her to the other helpers. They were a bit shy at first but soon found that this

Miss Cloud did not consider herself above the village women so it was easy to make friends in the bustle of activity.

When the rush was over Ann was free to go out and look for Richard. Simon Cloud came running up.

"I say Ann! I've had a super day! I spent all my money on horse rides. I rode the biggest one all round the field on my own twice."

Ann smiled at his excitement. "Hello Simon. What are you going to do now?"

"I'm not sure; but, what I want to know is, now I am on holiday, can I come and help you in your garden?" A voice behind him broke in.

"Simon, be so good as to introduce me to your friend."

Ann turned to find a tall woman with an excellently corseted figure, a thick matt complexion and large dark eyes. Her good looks were marred by lines of discontent from nose to mouth. As Simon remained silent the woman continued.

"You must be my husband's niece, Anastasia. Thank you for your kindness to Simon. Don't let him be a nuisance."

"But I enjoy having him," Ann was beginning when she saw Mrs Cloud's attention fixed on a group of people coming towards them. Bella and Mrs Dale escorted by Adrian and Mr Darcy were in the lead followed by Lady Kate and Lord David and Mr and Mrs Nebworth. Richard and Mary Heriot were hurrying along behind to join them.

"Very theatrical!" said Mrs Cloud.

Bella caught the tone and the look just as the band struck up with the unmistakable beat of the "Can-can". She flung off her hat, stepped sideways into the space between the groups, and launched into the traditional can-can routine complete with up-flung skirts showing black suspenders.

"Yippee!" shouted Adrian. He slid his arms out of his jacket and executed a circle of expert cartwheels round the dancing figure.

Surprise held the whole audience silent until the performance finished; then …

"Disgusting exhibition!" snorted Mrs Cloud as she turned away. "Come along Simon. It's time we went home." Her voice was drowned by the round of applause and Simon was too busy asking Adrian to teach him cartwheels to notice.

Ann heard a voice behind her say "What fun!" and turned to see a face with twinkling grey eyes and a wide smile, so like her father that she caught her breath.

"Who are you?" she asked. "You are so like my father."

"I've been told that before. I'm Bunty, your cousin. I have been longing to meet you."

Mrs Cloud addressed her daughter. "Elizabeth, will you please change back into your dress and come home with me."

The sparkle left the girl's face. She tossed her long fair plait. "I've been helping with the ponies so I had to wear jodhpurs. I can't come yet. I'll bring Simon home on the bus."

"Don't be late. I need you to help get ready for tomorrow's visitors."

"Oh lordy! Visitors tomorrow, and I wanted to come and see you at Cloud's End."

"I expect to be here all week. Come on Wednesday."

"I am sure we are going to be friends."

"Yes, I hope so."

"Now, will you all come back to the house," said Lord David. "I told Tom to announce the closing ceremony over the tannoy at 5.30."

"Are you going to announce our engagement?" asked Ann apprehensively.

"No, you are going to do that."

"I couldn't, in front of all these people."

"I think it is my job," said Richard. "So you don't have to worry."

When Ann was standing on the dais with Richard's arm round her waist she felt more confident. Lord David picked up the microphone.

"I know we do not usually have a closing ceremony but my friend Richard Brent would like to make a surprise announcement." He handed the mike to Richard who said:

"It's nothing very special. I just wanted to tell you that Ann Cloud has said she will marry me."

"Nothing very special!" spluttered Ann. "Is that how you feel about me?"

"No, of course not. But it is not special to all these people like it is to us."

This exchange came over the speaker and was clearly heard by everyone.

"Of course it's special," shouted a voice. "Let's give three cheers for Richard and Ann. Hip Hip ..." and the crowd joined in with enthusiasm.

"I hope you'll ask us all to the wedding," said Bill Jolly as he and his wife hurried up to be the first of many to congratulate the happy couple.

Later that evening when everything had been cleared away, Lady Kate invited the Nebworths and Mrs Dale and Mr Darcy to stay and have a snack supper.

"Well, seeing as Mr Nebworth has offered us a lift back to town, we would appreciate it very much," said Mrs Dale. "It could be a chance to have a chat with Richard. Just so as he knows that Ann is not completely without family."

"I hope I can join Ann's family," said Richard. "I'm very much on my own you know."

"Of course you can and welcome." The warmth of Auntie Lu's response was unmistakeable.

"You may not have family but you have plenty of friends," said Lady Kate.

"Yes," said Ann. "I was surprised how many people wanted to congratulate us."

"I thought my hand was going to fall off it was shaken so many times," added Richard.

Lady Kate summed up the situation.

"You have to remember that the union of two old established county families is very important to the village. We all hope you will have a long and happy life together.'

Chapter Twenty-two

"First thing you need to do is take down all this old ivy." Mr. Jolly was standing in front of Cloud's End talking to Ann. "Ivy takes a very strong hold. I'm afeared you may find a lot of damage. "

"I understand that but it has to be done."

"Mrs Cloud knew quite well. She should have had it taken down ten years ago but did not like to risk it."

"Will the whole house fall down?" asked Ann. Mr. Jolly was so gloomy that she feared the worst.

"No, there's no danger of that. We'll take it steady a bit at a time. What else do you want us to do?"

"Can you repair the roof over the old kitchen and fit a new secure door?"

"That should be no problem; but surely you don't intend to use it."

"Not as a kitchen but for storage. My grandmother left me her furniture. At present it is stored in the stable behind my uncle's office. I would like to store it here while the house is being repainted."

"Well, I can get the urgent jobs done now, but, after that, things will have to take their turn with other work I have on. It may be some time before I can get round to the inside."

"Of course, and I am very grateful for your help. How soon can I get new window frames?"

"That could be a problem. We're still suffering from the wartime wood shortage. I've used all my quota for this month and committed all I've got coming for months ahead."

"Oh dear! Will the glass fall out?"

"Let's have a look at the state they are in."

Ann followed him as he went round the house, examining the woodwork, poking doubtful places with his penknife and muttering to himself. Ann watched him and got more and more despondent. At last he spoke.

"They are not too bad. With a coat of paint now while they are dry and a bit of infill in places, these windows will hold together for some years yet."

"So that's it. Could you please give me some idea of what it is all going to cost, but get started on the ivy and the roof straight away."

"We've been hearing folks saying in the village that Mrs Cloud did leave you some money after all."

"Yes she did, but I don't want to spend it all at once."

"Very sensible, Miss, if I may say so. And now I must bid you good day."

As he turned to go a girl came cycling in from the road. "Good morning Miss Elizabeth," he said.

"All my friends call me Bunty." she said fiercely. "Are you my friend Mr Jolly?"

"I'm sure I hope so, Miss."

"Yes, and don't forget."

Mr Jolly got into his van and drove off leaving Ann and Bunty Cloud standing considering each other.

"I've brought sandwiches, so I can stay all day," said Bunty. "Where can I leave my bike?"

"Put it in the old kitchen," said Ann. "I've left mine there. Simon and his friend left theirs there too. Has he come with you?"

"No, not today. He has gone to Bournemouth with Julian Boscastle for a few days. He told me about your garden and I am longing to see it."

"It is very wild and I keep finding new and exciting discoveries. I've found gooseberry bushes absolutely laden with fruit. Mrs Bunch says they are a bit over-ripe but should be fine for making jam, which is easy to do now sugar is off the ration." Mrs Bunch had provided Ann with baskets and the girls spent a busy hour filling them with fruit.

"Mrs Bunch said I had to top-and-tail them," said Ann. "Shall we sit out in the garden and do that?"

"I'm hungry," announced Bunty. "Can we have our lunch first?" Ann made coffee and they sat on the steps sharing Bunty's sandwiches and Ann's biscuits. Then they got to work on the gooseberries preparing them for jam making. The monotonous job gave the cousins time to chat and get to know one another. Seldom could two girls have experienced such different environments in their formative years. Ann's description of the London elementary school; the commercial college where she learnt shorthand, typing and book-keeping, and her experiences working in London offices opened up a new world to Bunty, who was still at an all-girls boarding school.

"Your life sounds so interesting! I'm nearly sixteen and I've not done ANYTHING!"

"Do you think so?" Ann reviewed her life – getting up early, waiting for buses in all weathers, kept busy all day, arriving home tired and helping Auntie Lu with the washing up after the lodgers had finished their evening meal. "Most of the jobs were very boring."

"But – travelling round London on your own; knowing which bus to catch and passing all those famous old buildings! I never get out on my own in term time. I can cycle from home in the holidays but Mother always wants to know exactly where I am going. Simon has more freedom!"

"You are only sixteen. I am twenty one remember. I've been working for nearly seven years."

"Yes. You left school at fourteen. I am waiting for my School Cert results and then I expect I shall have to have another two years at school."

"Have you decided what you want to do?"

"I think I should quite like to be a vet."

"I believe that involves a long hard training. Perhaps you should try working for a vet to make sure you would like it."

"Oh thank you! It is so nice to be able to talk about real life. The girls at school are only interested in boys, clothes and make-up. My sister Emily is just as bad."

As she watched Bunty cycle off home Ann wondered if she were as much a misfit in her family as her own father had been with his mother and brother. But she did not realize how impressed Bunty had been with the 'romance' she had imagined in her cousin's life. Perhaps it was just as well she could not share Bunty's thoughts as she cycled home.

The following Monday morning Ann was talking to Mr Jolly who was helping one of his men start work on the ivy when Bunty arrived on her bicycle.

"Hello Mr. Jolly," she said.

"Good morning Miss – Bunty," he replied a bit hesitantly; mindful of her instructions but not quite sure that it would not get him into trouble."Whatever have you got on that bicycle of yours?"

Ann could understand his surprise. There were two bulky bags hanging either side the back wheel and a well-filled rucksack on Bunty's back . . .

"I've left home," she answered casually. "Come along Ann. I want to talk to you. Where can I dump all this clobber?"

"In the old kitchen the same as before. Then we'll go into the garden and eat our lunch. I'll put the kettle on. Would you like tea or coffee?"

"Anything will do; but not just yet. Do come along now."

Feeling as if she was being swept along by a storm Ann made a quick sortie into the house to collect her sandwiches and then joined Bunty on the terrace steps.

"Did you say you had left home?" she asked.

"Yes."

"Where are you going to live?"

"Here, with you."

"But you can't. There's no furniture."

"I thought you were living here with your cousin Bella."

"That was in June. We had to go back to London and took all the furniture back too. Anyway, we were only camping out on two camp beds."

"Oh dear! What shall I do? I'd better tell you."

"Tell me what?"

"I'm not going back to school. I want a proper life. I told the parents."

"What did they say?"

"There was a MONUMENTAL row!"

"So?"

"I did not appreciate all they had done for me and the expense of the best school all these years. I said I could have left school at fourteen and got a job. That would have saved the expense. They said I would have hated it."

"That's right. You would. I did. It was terrible!"

So then I went to see Mr Crane, the vet, and asked if I could be a nurse, or something, to help him with the animals. He said yes, and he'll pay me! Isn't that great!" Ann could not help wondering whether Mr Crane's co-operation was as much to defuse the Cloud family situation as a genuine need for help.

"You'll have something to live on then?"

"Yes. In a way I don't need it because Dad arranged a trust with some of my grandmother's money. I get interest paid into my account every month. But, if I go to university to learn to be a vet, I shall need a LOT of money. So every little helps."

"Surely you can live at home and cycle to Mallow Greening every day."

"No. That was the next thing! My Mother said that she was not prepared to see any child of hers working as a kennel girl and coming home smelling of animals every day. Dad said it was a waste to get such good results, six distinctions in School Cert. And not go into the sixth form for the Advanced level, which I would need for university. I said I could go to night school or day release at Commercial College. Then Mother said that was the end! If I wanted to associate with a lot of grubby little office girls I could leave home. I'm NOT going to be a kennel girl. I shall be a veterinary nurse." Ann could see that Bunty was almost in tears. Although her cousin seemed bold and self-confident she was really only a child. The row had upset her.

"So now we have to decide what we are going to do. If we go to London for a few days, which I was planning to do anyway, we can collect the camp beds and some other odds and ends. Then you can camp out with me for a bit."

"Where are you sleeping now?"

"I am staying with Mary Heriot. I am sure she will find you a bed for tonight.

"Oh thank you." Bunty seemed to have recovered. However Ann could not help wondering if Bunty's mother realized that, until recently, she, herself, had been one of those same scorned office girls.

Chapter Twenty-three

Ann was a little afraid that Mary Heriot would insist on Bunty returning home. However, after she had been told the whole story, she agreed to provide an extra bed and not make contact with Mr and Mrs Cloud. When supper had been eaten and cleared away Ann cycled down to Shallowford Farm to tell Richard what had happened and enlist his help to collect them and their luggage, including the two camp beds, at the end of the week.

"Mary was asking me if we had fixed a date for the wedding, and where it was going to be," said Ann a little shyly. She did not wish to appear in too much hurry.

"Well, it would be nice to have a week away for our honeymoon and I shan't be really free of the main farm jobs until the first week in October."

"That would make our wedding the first Saturday in October. Shall we go and ask Mr Heriot if that would be OK?"

"You want the service here at Mallow Greening?" He was surprised and added "I thought you would want to be married in London with your London friends."

"I have made so many friends here and I am sure that people like Auntie Lu and Mr and Mrs Nebworth would come and stay for the week-end. Besides, my parents were married in this church with all his friends and family, except his mother, joining them for the reception at the Bull afterwards."

"What about the house? Will Bill Jolly have it ready in time?" he was trying to be understanding, but she did not quite see what he meant.

"In time for what? Oh! I don't want to live there. It's much too big."

"So you'll be happy to come and live here at Shallowford?"

"Of course Richard. I thought that was what you wanted." She was puzzled. What was the problem?

"I just want you and I want you to be happy. Are you sure you don't want to go and live at Cloud's End?"

"Yes. I told you. It is too big. But, what I would like, if we can get it done in time, is to have our reception in the big downstairs rooms."

"That could be possible; but the first thing is to go and see the vicar and fix a date."

Next day in Mallow Greatham Bunty took charge. "We can leave our bicycles at the office," she said. "Put them here and I will tell Dad what we have done." She marched into the office and spoke to the receptionist.

"Good morning Dora. Is Dad free? This is my cousin Ann, Uncle Humphrey's daughter." Ann shook hands with the middle-aged woman who seemed to be very much in charge. She had lived in the area all her life and known Humphrey Cloud so that she was interested to see the new owner of Cloud's End. This girl seemed pleasant enough, but not particularly striking.

"Good morning Miss Cloud, pleased to meet you," she said. Then, turning to Bunty, "Mr Herbert has no-one with him at present Miss Elizabeth."

Ann followed Bunty up the stairs and into a long room with windows looking out onto the street.

"Hello, hello! What's up now?" asked Herbert Cloud briskly.

"Please Dad can we leave our bicycles in the yard? I'm going to London with Ann for a few days." Ann was surprised at Bunty's confident approach, but father and daughter seemed at ease with each other. Perhaps the mother was the problem.

"I thought you were going to stay at Cloud's End."

"There's no furniture. We have to get the camp beds from London."

"There is plenty of furniture here waiting to go back to Cloud's End."

"Yes please, and I would like to have it," said Ann. "I'm getting the old kitchen roof and door repaired and then I can store the furniture there until the rooms are ready to move it in."

"You will let me know when you are ready. Then I can have a clear-out," he said. Then, turning to his daughter, "If you are going to London you'd better give me your address. Your mother is sure to ask where you are."

Bunty had visited London before, travelling by taxi, calling at Harrods and the museums in Knightsbridge, so the London she saw with Ann was different. The bus was hot and crowded. The streets were dry and dusty, and the long street of flat-faced terrace houses seemed to go on for ever. At last they reached No. 25.

"Here we are," said Ann. "I wonder if Auntie Lu will be in? She will be surprised to see us!" She was indeed surprised and aghast at being required to provide an extra bed.

"Oh, Ann dearie! If you'd only let me know you were coming. I had a room empty all last week; just let it only last night. Not but what it's nice to see you dear, any friend of Ann's is more than welcome."

Bunty felt uncomfortable, but this was Ann's home.

"Never mind Auntie!" said Ann cheerfully. "We'll manage! Bunty can have my bed and I'll have one of the camp beds. There will just be room for it if we put the armchair out in the passage."

This idea of 'make-do' was strange to Bunty, as were the toilet arrangements.

"There is one bathroom on each floor except the attic," said Ann as they climbed the four flights of stairs. "There can be a bit of a queue in the mornings!"

Tea was also different. They had baked beans on toast followed by scones and fruitcake with tea to drink.

"Where's Bella?" asked Ann. "Is she working tonight?"

"Well, in a manner if speaking she is; but she is not getting paid for it."

"How's that?"

"That boy Adrian is in an amateur group that is putting on *Pygmalion* this week. The actress that was to play Mrs Pearce, the housekeeper, has sprained her ankle, so Adrian got round Bella on Monday and persuaded her to take the part at short notice. She has been studying it all week. Tonight is the dress rehearsal,"

"We must go and see it," said Ann. "Would you like that Bunty? I expect Bella can get tickets for us."

"And now tell me all the news," said Mrs Dale. "Have you and Richard fixed the date of the wedding? And where is it going to be? How about Brompton Old Church? That's very fashionable."

"Oh no Auntie! I could not bear a fashionable wedding. It is going to be at the little church at Mallow Greening the first Saturday in October. I'm hoping Bella will be my bridesmaid."

"I'm sure she would be happy to do so provided she is free. Are you going to wear white?"

"I would like to; if Bella agrees we will call on that stage dressmaker she knows and see about getting dresses made."

"Do you think ..." began Bunty... "Do you think I could be bridesmaid too?"

"Why yes, if you would like to, but Simon said you were bridesmaid at your sister's wedding and hated it."

"This would be different. I am sure you would let me choose my own dress without too many frills. It is so nice to have a cousin who is a real friend."

Next day they went by tube to Charing Cross so that Ann could show Bunty Trafalgar Square with the lion statues and the pigeons. Then they walked down Whitehall past the sentry sitting on his horse guarding the entrance to Horseguards. Bunty stood and stared.

"He must be very hot in that thick uniform," she said.

If the soldier heard her he gave no sign and continued to stare straight ahead. Then they came to the entrance to Downing Street followed by the Cenotaph.

"We shall soon be able to see the Houses of Parliament and Westminster Abbey," said Ann. "The best way to see London is on foot."

"There is so much history here," commented Bunty.

They had a late lunch in St James' park sitting on the grass and watching the ducks and then walked past Buckingham Palace to Victoria Station where they caught the tube back to No. 25.

In the evening they joined a theatre queue for "the gods".

"We always get the cheap tickets for the upper balcony," said Ann. It seemed strange to Bunty to be so far from the stage but she enjoyed the show.

And so the week progressed in a flurry of activity. When they went to see *Pygmalion* on the Thursday evening Adrian had a message for Ann.

"My uncle says can you come to the office tomorrow morning. He has had a letter from Herbert Cloud about the legacy."

"Is it confidential? Should I leave Bunty at home?"

"That's up to you, she is family after all!"

Bunty's comment was outspoken. "Is it about the money left you by my grandmother? I was away at school, so missed the rumpus when the parents heard about the codicil. But now I heard Dad say "It will be less of a drain on our funds if she will only accept.""

Chapter Twenty-four

Ann found out to what Mr Cloud had been referring when Mr Nebworth showed her the letter he had received from her uncle.

"As you see," he said. "Mr Cloud has sent you a cheque for four thousand pounds and says he has difficulty at present in raising the balance. So he suggests that, as you are going to marry Richard, you accept a parcel of a hundred acres of land which would increase the size of Richard's farm."

"So that's what he meant," exclaimed Bunty. "He got landed with that land when one of his clients went bust."

Ann looked at Mr Nebworth. "What do you think? I suppose I have to accept."

"Well, farm land in general fetches about fifty pounds an acre, so that could be said to fulfil his obligation."

"Why doesn't he sell it and give me the money?"

"Maybe it is not in good condition. It may not be very suitable for working with Shallowford Farm. Why don't you talk it over with Richard and see what he thinks?"

"If Richard does not want it then can I ask my uncle to sell it and give me the money?"

"You have a perfect right to make that decision," said Mr Nebworth and then he turned to Bunty. "I am sure you understand, Miss Elizabeth, that this is a confidential matter between Miss Ann Cloud and your father."

Richard's comment when Ann told him about the offer of land was short and to the point.

"The cheeky blighter! He is trying to cheat you Ann."

"Don't you want the land?"

"Well, it borders with your fields so would be reasonably easy to work with the farm but the land was overworked during the war and has been let go ever since. It would be years before I could make enough to pay you a reasonable rent for it."

"It would be 'ours' after we are married."

"You would be better off with the money properly invested."

Ann found difficulty in understanding Richard's problem about Herbert Cloud's offer of land and he refused further discussion.

"It is your problem," was all he would say.

"But, I don't know anything about land or farming," she protested.

"I can't help that."

She phoned Mr Nebworth to ask what she should do.

"Why don't you bring Richard here for Sunday tea? My wife will be delighted to see you both and we can discuss the problem informally."

"Thank you very much. That is very kind. I will ask Richard and let you know. Perhaps he will be able to get Tom Hoby to do the milking for him Saturday afternoon and Sunday so that we can come up to London for the week-end. I am sure my Aunt will find him a bed."

Saturday afternoon found them outside the door of No. 25. They were greeted enthusiastically by Mrs Dale.

"So nice to see you both. I am glad you were able to get away, Richard. I put clean sheets on the bed in No. 6, Ann. It's a student and he has gone home for the week-end so Richard can have his bed."

This "Box and Cox" arrangement was strange to Richard.

"Are you sure he won't mind?" he asked.

"No, of course not. You won't mess with his things, will you?"

Ann took him up the steep narrow stairs to room No. 6.

"Have you always lived here?" he asked.

"After my father died I could not live on my own so Auntie Lu was very good and gave me the attic bedroom. I had it for nothing until I started work and could pay her some rent."

"It sounds a bit limiting. Is it very small?"

"It is not very big but I was pleased to have it. You can come and see if you like."

"You don't think I meant …" he was embarrassed.

"Of course not. I trust you. Come and see."

Sunday morning was fine and sunny. They took sandwiches and went into Kew Gardens. Ann had planned to share her favourite places with Richard but, instead, they found a seat in a secluded spot and started to talk. Their talk ranged widely over their young lives commencing with day-to-day working routine and spreading to remembered childhood experiences. Inevitably Ann found herself describing life with her father. This encouraged Richard to talk about his father and touch on the devastation he felt when his father died.

"He must have been so miserable," he said. "My mother had died and I was away at school and could not help him. I still feel that I let him down."

"It wasn't your fault. How could you know? You were only a child," said Ann sensibly.

"I had to grow up overnight. Someone had to keep the farm going. There was only me. I left school and got stuck in. I guess I made a lot of mistakes."

"Couldn't you get anyone to help you?" asked Ann.

"Most of the men were away at the war. Lady Jane did what she could but she was snowed under with both James and David away."

"Anyway, you are now doing very well."

"Yes, I think I am winning, but it has been a hard struggle." He stared sombrely at the ground before him lost in his memories.

At last Ann could bear the silence no longer. She jumped up.

"Let's go and look at the pagoda. Then we can eat our lunch by the river and feed the swans."

All too soon it was time to leave the gardens and make their way to Wandsworth Common for tea with Mr and Mrs Nebworth. As they stood before the front door of the tall brick house Ann explained.

"Adrian has the top floor for his flat. Mrs Nebworth says the house is too big for just two people."

"I suppose London rents are very high," commented Richard. "But I would think he would find it difficult to be independent."

"It seems to work all right. He has his own kitchen and bathroom. Bella is there today. She is helping him cook his Sunday lunch."

There was no time for more. Mr Nebworth had opened the door and was welcoming them. Mrs Nebworth came bustling in from the kitchen.

"Tea's all ready. Come into the dining room. George, will you give a good bang on the gong to call Adrian and Bella. I should have thought they would have been down by now." As the boom of the big oriental gong echoed through the house Bella and Adrian came running down the stairs.

"Sorry! Are we late?" asked Bella.

"No, Richard and Ann have just arrived and tea is all ready."

As they ate their tea Ann told Mr and Mrs Nebworth about the work that Mr Jolly was carrying out at Cloud's End. She kept them amused with her description of going to bed with Bunty in the camp beds, which they had decided to put upstairs in a bedroom because Mr Jolly was working in the dining room. None of the lights would function! So they had to leave the hall light on all night. Ann asked Mr Jolly about this next morning.

"Well, of course, Miss," he said. "All the old wiring was disconnected when they did the new wiring downstairs."

"Whatever shall we do?"

"You could always take a candle to bed like they used to do in the old days," he suggested.

"Did you use candles?" asked Mrs Nebworth.

"No, we decided that was too old fashioned and we might start a fire so we bought a torch – two torches."

"Much more sensible." She turned to Richard. "I expect you had lamps and candles at the farm in the old days," she said.

"No, we always needed electricity for the farm so we had a generator until we were, eventually, connected up. But I remember our neighbours using oil lamps."

"I expect farming has changed a lot since the war," said Mr Nebworth. "How are you finding things?"

"I had a difficult job after my father died. I had to find out the hard way. Now I have got things sorted out and we are doing quite well."

"I suppose you had death duties to contend with as well as needing to finance the farm."

"Not so much that, the biggest difficulty was finding the cash to pay Mrs Cloud the rent for her fields. She insisted on being paid on time. I swore I would never let myself get in such a situation again."

"For that reason you are reluctant to take on the land that Herbert Cloud has offered to Ann."

"Yes. That land has potential, but over-production during the war took all the goodness out of it and it has just been left ever since. It needs re-seeding with grass and fertilizer before putting sheep or cattle on for a year or two. All the hedges are overgrown and have to be re-layed. It would be years before I was able to pay Ann any rent."

"But I should not want any rent."

"It is not right that you should have an investment that generates no income."

"What do you think I should do?"

"Get Herbert Cloud to do the honest thing and give you the cash."

"But he is my uncle."

"That's true," said Mr Nebworth. "I understand that family relations have been a bit strained in the past. You don't want to make things worse."

"Bunty and Simon are my friends."

"You would not want to make life difficult for them."

"Of course not."

"You and Richard are planning to get married and, I presume you will want to share things."

"I would like to share."

"Richard?"

"I don't quite see what you are getting at."

"Suppose you form a company and put all your assets – the farm and everything … "

"Don't forget my overdraft!" interjected Richard.

"OK, and overdraft. Then Ann could put in all her assets. Her existing land and this new holding."

"And the money my grandmother left me," said Ann.

Richard's "So!" was not very encouraging.

"Make it a Limited Company. You and Ann both be Directors and take a salary. Earned income attracts less tax than dividend payments."

"That's all very well! If you knew what I make from the farm …"

"Presumably spare cash goes on new equipment."

"Well – yes."

"You must be reasonably well equipped by now."

"I ought to get the barn roof re-tiled this year."

"How much land have you got?" asked Adrian.

"About a hundred and fifty acres, and all of it in good nick. I've put a lot of work into it over the last ten years."

"Would a farm of two hundred acres be a better bet?"

"Long term it would, yes, of course. No doubt about that."

Ann had been thinking. "I may not know much about farm work but I can do book-keeping and typing and filling in forms."

"I hate figures and form-filling," said Richard.

Mrs Nebworth had been listening to the discussion.

"It's a new idea and wants a lot of careful thought. Ann and Richard do you know each other well enough to work together as closely as that would mean? Husband and wife teams don't always work. I suggest you both think about it and, possibly, discuss the suggestion with a friend who could advise you."

"Such as Uncle Herbert!" broke in Bella, and the discussion ended in laughter.

"I will write to Herbert Cloud and say you are considering his offer," said Mr Nebworth.

"Are you going to ask him to the wedding?" asked Mrs Nebworth. "Bella tells me his daughter is going to be a bridesmaid."

"Yes, Bunty and I have become great friends."

"Will her parents expect to be asked?"

"Now see what you have let yourself in for!" said Richard.

"Oh Richard ! Would you mind very much if they came?"

"They are your nearest relations after all," said Mrs Nebworth.

"You'll be pleased to know I have not got any relations to worry about," said Richard.

Chapter Twenty-five

The next excitement was the arrival of the furniture. Bunty had just returned from her duty at the morning animal clinic when the big van drew up by the front door.

"Where are you going to put all grandmother's furniture?" she asked.

"Whose furniture is it?" wondered Ann to herself. "Grandmother's or mine – or does it really belong to the house?" There was no time to speculate further the driver had got down from his cab and was waiting to speak to her.

"Good morning Miss. Can you tell us where you want all this furniture?" They went round to the back of the van. Piled on top of the load was a table with chairs nestled between the legs.

"Well, I want most of it put in the big old back kitchen so that I can sort it out; but those chairs and the table can go in the hall." So the table and chairs were unloaded. Then the van backed round to the kitchen door and item after item of heavy Victorian furniture was carried in until there was barely room to pass between them even with certain lighter items stacked on top.

As Ann was watching in amazement the driver came up to her, "We've got some beds next, Miss. Do you want them in here as well?"

"No; those would be better upstairs. Can you manage to take them up?"

"No problem!" So the solid wooden bed-heads and the sprung metal frames were taken up and assembled.

"That's good!" said Bunty. "We shan't need to sleep on the camp beds any more."

"They are no good without mattresses and blankets!" As she was speaking mattresses were being carried up the stairs and put on the beds. "I suppose we shall find blankets in one of the chests." Sure enough, the blankets were found and hung out in the sunshine to air.

At last all that was left in the van was a wall of tea chests at the far end.

"Where do you want these cases, Miss?" asked the man

"I wonder what is in them?" she said.

"You'll have to open them to see, but some are very heavy and could be books."

"Books! I can't wait to see! Please put them in the hall where there is space to look at them."

After the men had climbed back into the cab and the van had driven away, the girls stood looking at the cases. "How do we get them opened?" wondered Ann.

"Shall I go and find Mr Jolly?" asked Bunty. "He should be able to take the lids off." Before she could turn to go there was an exclamation behind them.

"Look at the state that furniture's in! I knew as you was going ter need me!" The unmistakeable tones made them swing round as Nellie Crouch emerged from the passage to the old kitchen.

"Hello Nellie, do you know what is in these cases?" asked Ann.

"I may do and I may not. It wasn't me that was asked to help pack up Mrs Cloud's things when the house was shut up after she had died." It was evident she intended to wait and see them opened up. Ann was trying to find the right words to tell her to go away when Bunty returned with Mr Jolly.

"You want these cases opened?" he asked. "Do you know if they contain breakables?"

"She had some nice china," said Nellie. "Good stuff it was! Wouldn't let me touch it 'case I broke some."

"OK, I'll take it steady."

Ann and Bunty watched while he prised open the tops of the cases. There were books, and boxes of china and glass wrapped in newspaper for protection. On top of the last one was a framed picture wrapped in brown paper. Ann undid the parcel and found a portrait of a young girl painted in the style of a late nineteenth century debutante. She was not exactly beautiful but very elegant and looked out of the picture with the smiling confidence of one whom life had always treated well.

"What a lovely picture," said Ann. "I wonder who it is?"

Nellie Crouch spoke from behind them. "That's Mrs Cloud before she was married. Picture used to hang over the fireplace in the drawing room."

"We must put it back when the room is ready," decided Ann.

"I'll be glad to help you put the room to rights after that Bill Jolly and his men have messed it up."

Ann looked at her smiling. "Will you do that?" she asked.

"Yes – and there is all that furniture to be cleaned and polished, bin left in that dirty damp old coach-house all this time! Terrible state it's in! Two mornings a week I'll come, that's all I can manage. Tuesdays and

Thursdays – will that do you? You pay me what's fair. I'll not cheat you!" She turned and marched out of the front door. Ann breathed a sigh of relief. She found Nellie a bit overpowering. Then she turned back to that last case. There were photograph albums that had been packed in underneath the painting.

"Have you seen these before?" Ann asked Bunty.

"No." she replied. "Do you think there are pictures of the family?"

Who can resist the chance to see what their elders were like when young? The albums were soon spread out on the table. The cousins sat side by side and opened the first one. There was a picture of a fine Palladian mansion.

"I've seen that before," said Bunty. "It is Drum House. Lord Drumheller lived there. I think he was grandmother's uncle, she grew up there."

"Why was that?" asked Ann.

"I can't quite remember. I think there was a divorce or her mother died, something like that."

They turned the page and there was a family group posed in front of the same house. In the centre was the patriarch with luxurious curly hair and beard, his top hat resting on his knee; beside him was an elegant lady with leg-o-mutton sleeves and large hat. There were four young men standing behind them and two girls sitting on the steps in front.

"I think one of those girls must be grandmother," said Bunty.

As they turned the pages they saw the same two girls. They were grouped beside a sundial, driving in a pony trap, riding side-saddle in full hunting dress complete with top hat and posing in elegant ball gowns. They began to see the resemblance to the face in the portrait.

"Yes, this one is definitely grandmother," said Bunty. Ann could not help but agree. "She must have had a fabulous life," she said.

Then, as they continued going through the albums, they saw photos of weddings with the two cousins as bridesmaids. A studio portrait of their grandmother as a bridesmaid showed a tenseness in the poise figure and a frown between the dark eyebrows.

"Coming to live at Cloud's End must have seemed rather a comedown after such a luxurious childhood," said Bunty. "Look! Here's a wedding photo outside our church. That is Grandpapa, I remember him,"

Ann studied the photo. He was smiling at his bride; she was staring straight ahead. Ann thought she did not look as radiantly happy as a bride should, she felt sympathy with her grandmother and wondered whether she had hoped that her eldest son would marry into the society that she had left. Was that the reason for her reaction to Humphrey's wish to marry an actress? She was never going to know. It was ancient history now. Better to forget it. She looked at her watch.

'"Goodness me! Look at the time!" she said. "Let's get lunch quickly so that I can go out and do some more work in the garden."

They piled the photo albums back in the box and took up their normal activities.

Chapter Twenty-six

It was a cool evening for early September. Janet Crane had lighted a fire and was sitting beside it reading a letter, which she then crumpled up and tossed into the fire just as Bunty came in.

"Clinic finished early this evening," she said. "So I thought I would come for a chat. Are you busy writing letters?"

"No. These are old ones. I'm throwing them away."

"Are they love letters?" The girl's curiosity was too naive to offend.

"Not really. Just letters from Patrick."

"You were engaged to him and then he was killed."

"Yes. How did you know?"

"There was a girl from school knew his family. We all thought it so sad."

"It hurt at the time; but life has to go on."

"So you are going to burn his letters?"

"That's right."

"Please may I watch? It's so romantic!"

What could Janet say? To object would make it seem so much more important. She nodded her head and, silently, one by one, the letters were crumpled up and put on the fire.

"I'm surprised you are not stopping to read any of them."

"There's no point." Of course, had she been on her own she would have read every one; but, it was surely better this way.

As the last one went up in flames Bunty heaved a deep sigh. "Oh-h! I do think you are brave! Now I must go."

After Bunty had left Janet sat on deep in thought. She and Patrick had lived near and grown up together. It had been a big break when he was called up. Would their life together have been happy? That was something she would never know. Several large tears trickled down her cheeks. Just then Lord David came in and caught her unawares.

"Oh I say! Are you all right?" This was not the brisk, business-like Janet he was used to seeing.

Janet wiped her eyes. "I'm OK thanks."

"Something's wrong," he saw the debris on the fire. "You have been burning letters. Is there a problem? Can I help?"

"No, not really. They are just Patrick's letters to me. There was no point in keeping them after all this time."

"I suppose you have been reading them all, and it has brought back your grief!"

"No," she gave a slight laugh. "I had just started when Bunty Cloud came in, she asked if she could watch, seemed to think it so romantic! I could not read them with her watching. I suppose it was better really!"

"Much better." He considered her for a moment. She had kept very busy with the Guides, WI and all the other village activities but maybe her loss had gone deeper than he thought. Was she ready for a new relationship? Not just yet perhaps. Better tell her why he had come.

"I called in to see if you and your father were free on Saturday. My mother thinks it would be nice to have a small dinner party for the engaged couple, Ann and Richard. Edward and Mary Heriot are coming. It could be an opportunity to make sure the arrangements for the wedding are all in hand."

"How very kind. Just wait while I check Father's diary. I am pretty sure he is free." Janet was her usual brisk self again.

On Saturday Ann and Richard were the last to arrive. Lady Kate sensed tension between them. Ann's eyes looked a bit moist. They both accepted glasses of sherry and joined in the conversation. As they sat down at the table Lady Kate commented.

"I hear that Bunty Cloud is living with you at Cloud's End, Ann. What is she doing tonight?"

"She has gone to the cinema with Andy."

"I gave her a job working with small animals when she told me she had refused to go back to school," said Mr Crane. "I thought it would keep her out of mischief."

"She says she intends to train as a vet," added Janet. "I must say she has some original ideas!"

"How is that?" asked the vicar.

"You know Mrs Lavine?" said Mr Crane.

"The overweight lady with her fat spaniel."

"Yes. She was concerned about Poggy Paddy's breathlessness and brought him in for consultation. Bunty took over."

"I hope she was tactful." Said Lady Kate.

"She asked about his diet and how much exercise he had and shook her head solemnly over the answer," said Janet. "Just give him half a tin tonight, nothing else. Make sure he has plenty of water. I will come and see about his food in the morning. Can I have breakfast with you?"

"What did Mrs Lavine say?"

"'Of course my dear, what would you like? Bacon, sausage, fried egg, mushrooms?' I think she is lonely."

"The lady always enjoys her food. What did Bunty say to that?"

"I never have anything cooked, thank you. Cornflakes, toast and an apple will be fine."

"What happened?"

"Of course Mrs Lavine was too polite to indulge in her usual 'blow-out'. She did say 'Poor Paddy is missing his bacon and sausage!' Then Bunty took both owner and pet for a walk. She intends to carry on the treatment for a week."

"I heard her telling Andy. 'The poor dog was sitting begging all through the meal. I'm sure she gives him scraps!'"

"What does she expect?" asked Lady Kate. "The dog is company for a lonely lady."

"She is also friendly with the Herbert Clouds," said Lord David. "I hope she gives them a good account of Bunty's activities."

"That's good," said Ann. "I think she was shattered by her mother's anger when she told them she was not going back to school."

"So she came to stay with you?"

"Yes, we get on very well. It is interesting to hear her talk. At her age I had been out at work for nearly two years."

The short silence that followed that statement was broken by Lord David.

"How is Jolly getting on with the jobs at Cloud's End?"

"He has removed all the ivy, got the roof repaired and fitted a new door to the old kitchen."

"You surely don't need to use that."

"I need somewhere to store the furniture."

"Mrs Cloud's furniture?"

"Yes. I had it delivered last week. The kitchen is jam packed full!"

"What are you going to do with it?"

"It has to be cleaned and polished. Nellie Crouch turned up and told me it must be done properly. So she is coming two mornings a week. I have also got her husband, Tom, coming to help me in the garden."

"He's not good for much more than digging."

"That's what I thought, but he has shown me how to prune the gooseberries and cut back the raspberries so that I shall have a good crop next year."

"You're infatuated with that garden," said Richard.

"Why not? I never had a garden before." She seemed a little on the defensive. Lady Kate asked whether there was a good crop of apples and the conversation continued in general chat about the harvest and plans for the Harvest Festival in church.

At the end of the meal Lord David stood up. "I ask you to raise your glasses to Richard and Ann and wish them a very happy wedding day."

"I don't know that there is going to be a wedding day!" said Ann.

"What!!" Everyone including Richard stared at her in consternation. He was the first to find his voice.

"Whatever do you mean? You can't let me down now!"

"Every time I try to talk to you about this offer from Uncle Herbert you clam up and won't discuss it. We can't go on like that."

"What offer is this?" asked Lady Kate.

"He is trying to pull a fast one and swindle Ann, and I won't have it!"

"How is this?" asked Lord David. "Surely Herbert Cloud would not suggest anything dishonest."

"It's very close to it," said Richard darkly.

"Just let me explain," said Ann. "You know that the codicil of my grandmother left me ten thousand pounds."

"And that put Herbert in a bit of difficulty," commented Lord David.

"Now he has sent me a cheque for four thousand pounds in addition to the thousand I already have and asked if I would accept a hundred acres of land as settlement for the balance."

"What land is this?" asked Lord David.

"It is called Paradise," said Ann.

"You know. It runs alongside the Cloud's End property," added Richard. "It is not bad land but it has been badly let down."

"I thought that Richard could add it to his farm."

"And I say it is not a good investment of five thousand pounds!"

"I don't know," said Lord David. "Land values are low now but I can see them appreciating over the next ten or twenty years. It could be a very good investment."

"Mr Nebworth suggested that we form a limited company with Richard and me as paid directors," explained Ann.

"Sounds good to me. What's the problem?"

"To run a bigger unit we would need more working capital."

"I've got four thousand pounds."

"And I've got an overdraft. Forget it!"

"I can sympathize with Herbert Cloud," said Lord David. "He got most of his mother's money tied up before he knew about this. Do you want to accept this land Ann?"

"Yes, I think it would help him and also, long term, it would be nice for Richard to have a bigger farm."

"Thank you very much!" said Richard sarcastically.

"Can I help you to look at the financial details?"

"We have a meeting with Adrian next week. I'd be glad if you could be there," said Richard.

Ann's quiet "Thank you Richard." Showed how much she appreciated this concession.

Chapter Twenty-seven

Ann was in a hurry. She wanted to pick some apples to take down to Shallowford Farm before the meeting they had with Adrian and David. Nellie Crouch claimed her attention.

"Can yer come and give me a 'and, Miss Ann?"

Ann followed her into the big kitchen. There was more space since the big dresser had been moved into the dining room the previous day. She found Nellie standing in front of the big bureau with the tall bookcase mounted upon it.

"What's the problem?"

"Look! The curtains for the big room are in this drawer. They're creased bad. Need to be hung out." Ann abandoned the idea of apples and bent down to help lift the heavy green velvet curtains out of the big drawer. First one and then the other was taken outside, given a good shake and hung over the clothes line.

As she was closing the drawer Ann noticed a parcel at the back. It was an old shoebox tied up with string. "That's strange," she said. "It says "To be given to Richard Brent after January 1st 1953." I better take it down and give it to him." A thought struck her. Did you know it was there Nellie?"

"Nothing t'do with me what the old lady does, Miss. Queer ideas her had towards the end. Very 'ard on Mister Richard she was."

Ann hurried off to put the box in her bicycle basket and set off for her meeting at the farm. She found Adrian and David sitting at the long table in the kitchen with Richard.

"Look what I've found, Richard," she said as she dumped the box on the table in front of him.

"What's this?" he asked

'It's got your name on it. Aren't you going to open it?'

He untied the string and took off the lid. "Well I'll be blowed!" he exclaimed. The box was full of ten pound notes. On top was a sheet of paper. He picked it up and read.

"I herewith return to Mr Richard Brent the rents paid for use of my land with congratulations on the success of his efforts. Signed Emily

Cloud. So that's why she always insisted on my always paying her in cash!" he said as he started to count the money.

Lord David turned to Adrian. "As Mrs Cloud's estate has been settled for some time I think we should keep quiet and not mention this outside these four walls."

"A bit irregular! But I'm prepared to go along with that," he replied.

Richard had finished counting. "Four hundred pounds!" he said. "Eight years' rent!"

Ann gasped! "Four hundred pounds! And I brought it down here in my bicycle basket," she exclaimed.

The men laughed. "What did you think was in it?" asked David.

"I don't know. Some kind of souvenirs; photographs perhaps! What are you going to do with the money?"

"I shall use two hundred pounds to pay off my overdraft and the rest as a wedding present to you, Ann."

"What do you mean?"

"It gives me something to put into this company that Adrian has suggested. You put two hundred pounds and the land from Herbert Cloud and I put this and my land. That's fair!"

"Are you sure?" Ann could hardly believe the difficulties to be over.

Richard put his hand over hers as Lord David said "that sounds a very good solution to me. With that as a rough basis I am sure Adrian can help us put together a working arrangement."

When Adrian left after lunch Ann took a deep breath and said to Richard.

"I hope you understood all that. I am sure I shall never remember everything."

"Don't worry. It's early days yet. We just carry on and get married."

"Yes," she said blissfully.

After he had finished kissing her she turned to business.

"Now we must send out the invitations."

"Do we really have to ask Herbert Cloud and his wife?"

"Oh, I think so. He is my uncle and Bunty is a bridesmaid. I'm going to be living here. I can't offend him."

"I have asked David to be my Best Man."

"And Uncle Fred Darcy is going to give me away; then there are the vicar and Mary Heriot and Janet and her father."

"Should we ask Andy?"

"Oh yes. He is Bunty's friend. He can be an usher and Simon can help him. Mr and Mrs Nebworth have promised to come, they can stay at the White Hart. Adrian is going to bring Bella on Friday evening." Ann counted up on her fingers, "That makes sixteen with Lady Kate and Auntie Lu."

"Do you still want to hold the reception at Cloud's End?"

"Yes. Mr Jolly has almost finished the downstairs rooms. Now I can get the furniture polished and moved in."

"Do you intend to ask Bill Jolly?"

"Oh yes. We must have Mr and Mrs Jolly. He has been so helpful right from the beginning."

During the next few weeks they were both very busy. Richard was working long hours to get the harvest in and secure. Ann caught up with him for brief spells to report progress. The wedding was planned for 3 p.m. Lady Kate had organized a meeting with Ann, Mrs Bunce and Harriet to discuss the menu for the reception buffet. Mrs Bunce and Harriet were thrilled to be asked to help with the preparation and to serve at the reception.

"It's so long since we had a wedding in the village,' said Harriet.

"I'm so happy for Mr Richard,' sighed Nannie Bunce.

"Do you think I should ask Nellie Crouch to help with the washing up?' asked Ann.

"There's no reason why not," said Lady Kate. "But don't worry if she says no. One never knows how Nellie will take things."

Everything worked out according to plan. On the eve of the great day Ann and Bunty, who were staying at the castle at Lady Kate's invitation, were joined by Bella, who had been given a lift by Adrian.

"It's all right," said Bella as she staggered in with a pile of dress boxes. "He has booked a room at the White Hart. Mr and Mrs Nebworth will be staying there tomorrow night. I was really grateful not to have to bring all the dresses on the train."

"Richard has invited me to his 'Stag Night'," said Adrian. "It all fitted in very nicely. Tho I wouldn't say no to a nice cup of tea if I was offered one!"

Chapter Twenty-eight

Mary Heriot was standing at the back of Mallow Greening church. She was pleased with the results of the morning's work. The little church was full of flowers from all the gardens in the village. There was a mixture of autumn colours from vivid purple asters and michaelmas daisies to yellow, orange and deep red chrysanths. Any 'flower arranger' would have been horrified by the clashes of colour, but she had welcomed all the villagers' offerings. She was amazed at their goodwill as they ransacked their gardens for the best blooms; and now they had come to fill the church for the ceremony. It seemed that Ann had become part of the community and overcome the hostility felt to old Mrs Cloud.

The groom and best man had already arrived and were standing waiting for the bride. Richard looked so smart and handsome in the formal outfit that Mary hardly recognized him. She decided that Lady Kate's efforts had been truly crowned with success. His dark hair had been cut and slicked down flat; his face had a healthy tan from his open air life; the bitter lines of tension in his face seemed to have been smoothed out by happiness. Mary offered a little prayer for Ann in the hope that she would be able to keep him happy.

Then Ann came into the church. She wore a long cream dress and carried a bouquet of peach coloured roses out of her garden. These matched the peach of the bridesmaids' dresses, which were the fashionable 'new look' style with calf-length flared skirts and V neck finished at the back by a bow with long ribbon streamers dangling down. The dressmaker had told them that these were called "*Suivez moi jeune homme*!" but thought that was only in France.

Bella had used her theatrical skill with make-up. A touch of mascara and eye-shadow emphasized the sparkle in Ann's eyes. Bunty was a bit scornful, but, after Bella had combed out her honey-coloured hair and applied a little make-up to eyes and lips she decided she really looked quite "grown up".

The Reverend Ernest took the service quietly and sincerely. He commented on the pleasure he felt in joining two members of old established local families and acknowledged the support provided by local residents who filled the church. Then he read the well-known passage from St Paul's Epistle to the Corinthians, which defines love or charity.

"My good friends," he said. "Our love of God and our love for our neighbour should always be the guiding principles in our lives."

The bride and groom made their responses clearly and positively and the register was signed.

While the photographs were being taken outside the church, Harriet and Ivy Bunch hurried back to Cloud's End where the buffet was set out on the big table in the dining room. They put sausage rolls and quiches to heat, removed covering cloths from the sandwiches and salad and put fresh logs on the fires. Then they filled the glasses set out on the sideboard with red and white wine. As they worked they talked.

"Wasn't it a lovely service," said Ivy. "I am so happy for Mr Richard. He has been alone for so long."

"You'll find life a bit different with a 'mistress' in the house."

"I'm sure things will work out well. If I know Miss Ann she will spend all her time in her garden."

"I heard her telling Lady Kate that she planned to help local farmers with their forms and paperwork."

"Maybe she will; but perhaps there will be babies coming along and that will keep her busy."

"You will enjoy having babies to look after."

"Indeed I will. It seems only a short time since Mr Richard was a happy little lad before all the troubles came along."

"You'll find the farm a bit crowded."

"There is always Cloud's End waiting for us to move in to."

"I wonder when that will be! Now everything is ready and I think I hear people arriving."

The reception went well. Lady Kate and her helpers were congratulated on the spread which some said was almost pre-war standard. The usual speeches were made and healths drunk; the guests formed little groups and sat chatting. Lady Kate took the opportunity to go upstairs, visit the bathroom and have a look at the bedrooms. Although she had visited Mrs Cloud from time to time she had never been upstairs before. She came down the stairs looking thoughtful. Then her attention was caught by Mr Herbert Cloud who was speaking to Mr Nebworth.

"Of course she should have sold the house. I have to tell you I consider she was very badly advised." Mr Nebworth firmly refuted this criticism.

"Perhaps you have not been told that I had prepared a Power of

Attorney authorizing me to sell all ready for Miss Cloud to sign and she refused. It was her prerogative."

"Oh well! I suppose you had to accept her decision. And now I hear that she and Richard plan to set up a limited company. Do you think that is a wise move?"

"It may seem a bit unusual but I am sure you will see many similar arrangements set up in future."

"In London I expect you have a more modern ..." Lady Kate's attention was caught by Mrs Cloud who was talking to Mrs Nebworth.

" ... and another thing, she has had such a subversive influence on Elizabeth."

Mrs Nebworth turned her head to look at Bunty, to whom she had chatted earlier in the evening.

"Is that your daughter? I do think she looks charming. That colour and style of dress is just right for her."

"I had nothing to do with it. I think it is much too severe."

"Don't you think it will be ideal for 'hops' and dances when she goes to Veterinary College. I had a long chat with her. It is nice when a girl has a definite objective in life."

"In my opinion training girls is a waste if time and money. They always get married." Just then she saw Bunty come out of the dining room. "It's getting late; past the children's bedtime. Elizabeth, we're going home. Can you find Simon and come along."

"We can't come yet. Bella and Adrian are doing an entertainment for us."

"How will you get home?"

"I am sure Andy will give us a lift."

"In that ramshackle open sports car! You'll catch your death of cold!"

"Perhaps we can help." Mrs Nebworth smiled at Bunty. "We are spending the night at the White Hart and can easily see the young people safely home."

Mrs Cloud had to accept this offer. "Thank you. I hope you will not find it too much trouble. Now, come along Herbert; we must say goodbye to Richard and Ann."

Mr and Mrs Cloud made their farewells and drove away. Ann and Richard stood outside the house savouring the quiet and freshness of the autumn evening.

"Oh Richard! I'm so happy," said Ann.

"Oh, my darling, so am I," he said as he put his arms round her and pulled her close to him. "Sweetheart!" he said as he dropped a gentle kiss on the top of her head.

Bunty found Andy teasing Simon.

"You're looking very smart, young fellow!"

"Do you think so?" he replied. "I had this outfit for Emily's wedding. Mother insisted that I wore it again." He looked down at the white shirt, maroon silk waistcoat and bow tie to match. "Seems a bit sissy to me!"

Bunty giggled. "He couldn't wear the trousers. They were much too short. Those are his best school ones."

"I would rather wear jodhpurs."

"Well, why not? I here and now give you permission to wear jodhpurs at my wedding," said Andy.

"OK, thanks. By that time I should be a top jockey."

"Riding races is awfully hard work. Why don't you train for a vet like Bunty?"

"Don't put him off. Just let my mother hear of it. She'll begin to think that my being a vet is the least of the evils."

In the sitting room Lady Kate found four men relaxing. They had managed to acquire a glass of beer each. Mr Darcy was talking to the vicar.

"I liked your talk, Padre, it reminded of when I was a kid and went to Sunday school."

"Did it? I hope it provided food for thought both for the young couple and others in the congregation."

"Yes," said Mr Crane. "Richard is apt to say what first comes to mind without thinking."

"We must hope that Ann understands and will help him."

"Oh! Richard is a good lad," broke in Bill Jolly. "I am sure Miss Ann understands. – Now Mr Heriot, what do you want me to do about the leaves in the church gutters?"

Mrs Dale was talking to Mary Heriot and Mrs Jolly.

"You know, I would never have thought that Ann would be married before Bella. All out in the country too – such a different life! I do hope she will be happy."

"I am sure she will," said Mary. "She enjoys country life. I will always remember how her face lit up when she first took me out to look at her garden."

"And the house," said Mrs Jolly. "Bill has been really impressed at the business-like way she has planned work on this house."

Mrs Dale was still worried. "Do you really think she will settle and be happy? After all she has only known this boy, Richard, for six months, and we are so far away."

"Yes I know, but we live quite close," said Mary. "Be sure I shall keep an eye on them. She has so much to give to Richard. He has relaxed and is quite a different person."

Lady Kate turned to Ann, who was standing in the sitting room, wondering who she should talk to next. She found this social business a bit wearing.

"My dear, you have done wonders getting these rooms refurbished," she said.

Ann looked round. "It can never be as nice as your room at the castle, but I am glad you approve. I have enjoyed planning it out."

"How much more is there to do to the house before it is finished?"

"All the upstairs has been rewired and now must be decorated. The old bathroom has to be completely stripped and new units fitted. I made it as nice as I could so that it could be used today but it really is rather grotty."

"I suppose getting a new bath and washbasin etc will be difficult."

"Mr Jolly says it may be a year, especially as I want yellow and not white."

Lady Kate thought for a minute, her eyes on Lord David, who was sitting talking quietly to Janet Crane. "I'm hoping David will get married one day," she said. "Then I shall want somewhere to live. Would you be prepared to rent me the house?"

Ann was surprised. "Would you like it? But it needs so much doing – and the stables are really dangerous."

"Yes, I should need to stable my horses. But there is no hurry. Keep it to yourself. Don't say anything to David."

"David and Janet? Do you really think …?"

"I may be wrong. We have to wait and see."

Ann realized that further comment would not be welcomed.

"Here come Bella and Adrian. They have an idea for a short entertainment. If you'll excuse me I must tell everyone to bring their chairs in here and make sure that Harriet and Nannie Bunch don't get left out."

When everyone was suitably seated Bella stood up. Adrian was seated by her with his guitar.

"Let me just explain," said Bella. "We had thought we might perform a short excerpt from *As You Like It*, but there was nothing suitable, so I shall start by singing a song from the play, which I think is quite appropriate."

She sang 'There was a lover and his lass' with guitar accompaniment by Adrian. After that they sang a folk song with questions and replies.

Then Adrian recited the poem, 'The Jackdaw of Rheims', with graphic actions as he went through the story of the Jackdaw that stole the Lord Cardinal's ring and was cursed by 'Bell, Book and Candle'. Which was followed by Bella singing some popular songs including 'Somewhere over the Rainbow'.

Then it was Adrian's turn. He struck a chord on his guitar and started to sing:

"Did you not see my lady, go down the garden singing?
Blackbird and thrush were silent to hear the alleys ringing.
But, did you not see my lady out in the garden there?
Rivalling all the sunbeams, with a glory of golden hair."

Then he put down his guitar and stepped forward, smiling a little sheepishly. He put out a hand to pull Bella to her feet as he said, "I won't sing the second verse because it would not be true. I am delighted to be able to tell you that Bella has promised to marry me."